HOA WIRE

KENNETH EADE

Times Square Publishing
Copyright 2015 Kenneth Eade

ISBN: 1507862288/ISBN 13: 978-15078622885

ASIN: B00QPD8HF6

All rights reserved. No part of this book may be reproduced or transmitted in any form or by any means, electronic or mechanical, including photocopying, recording, or by any information storage and retrieval system, without permission in writing from the publisher. Reviewers may quote brief passages in the context of a review.

This is a work of fiction. Names, characters, places, and incidents either are the product of the author's imagination or are used fictitiously, and any resemblance to actual persona, living or dead, business establishments, events or locales is entirely coincidental. The publisher does not have any control over and does not assume any responsibility for author or third-party Web site or their content.

The scanning, uploading and distribution of this book via the Internet or any other means without the permission of the publisher is illegal and punishable by law. Please purchase only authorized electronic editions, and do not participate in or encourage electronic piracy of copyrighted material.

OTHER BOOKS BY KENNETH EADE

Brent Marks Legal Thriller Series

A Patriot's Act

Predatory Kill

Unreasonable Force

Killer.com

Absolute Intolerance

Involuntary Spy Espionage Series

An Involuntary Spy

To Russia for Love

Non-fiction

Bless the Bees: The Pending Extinction of our Pollinators and What You Can Do to Stop It

A, Bee, See: Who are our Pollinators and Why are They in Trouble?

Save the Monarch Butterfly

For my wife, Valentina, the best person to have in my corner

"Homeowner's Association: the means whereby people who own homes are able to transfer their rights to the neighborhood control freaks."

-Ron Brackin

CHAPTER ONE

Orange Grove was a pleasant modern community in Goleta, California. A former orange orchard, it was a small development, with fresh air and rolling hills. Four different models of tract townhomes, one attached to the other, repeated themselves in different combinations to line twelve perfectly manicured cul-de-sacs. Breezy blues, avocado greens, tilled tans, and cozy creams decorated the exterior of the nearly identical rows of houses, and filled the sleepy bedroom community with a pleasant palette chosen by the developer. Driveways sculpted within twin patches of green led to automatic rollup aluminum garage doors. At a touch of a button, you drove into your garage. At another touch of a button, you were greeted by the soft lights of your own private sanctuary, your castle.

Barbara Densmore was a busybody. Ever since she had learned how to use her nose, she had a terrible habit of sticking it into everyone's business. Growing up, she was always on this or that student committee, and, due to her big mouth and ability to influence people weaker than she was, she was elected head of the student body council at Santa Barbara High School. Barbara had many acquaintances, but no friends to speak of; nobody who would really stick their neck out for her in time of need. Nevertheless, for a resident living in Orange Grove, staying on Barbara's good side was the best way to avoid a tremendous headache.

Today was Barbara's birthday. She could expect a call from her mother, of course, but she and her sister had not spoken in over fifteen years. Barbara had stolen away her sister's boyfriend, Stan, and her sister, Joyce, had never had it in her heart to forgive either one of them. Barbara and Stan had been divorced now for about five years, but that still had not changed the chilly air between her and Joyce.

Barbara entered the small development, and drove the streets, waved to the neighbors who were out in their yards and stopped to chat with some of them. But her real motivation was to find violators of the HOA rules. She had, of course, memorized all of the pesky rules, and kept a little notebook to make notes of whose lawn was overgrown, who left too many cars parked in the driveway, and who had changed the color of their curtains. Today was a non-eventful day. There were the usual infractions that had not yet been abated, but other than that, it was a picture of perfect compliance.

"Happy birthday Barbara!" called out Frances Templeton, the VP of the homeowner's association, as Barbara drove by. Barbara stopped to chat with Frances for a while, finished her rounds, and pulled in to the driveway of her perfectly compliant townhome.

Barbara parked her white Toyota Prius in the driveway, and walked up the beautifully tailored walkway to her front door. On the porch was an exquisite bouquet of red roses wrapped in cellophane, with an impressive red ribbon tied around the vase. Attached to the plastic wrap was a card. Barbara smiled, and opened the card. It read, "To a dear neighbor."

Barbara lifted the bouquet into her arms, opened the door, walked in, and set it down on her kitchen table. *There must be two dozen roses here*, she thought. *I wonder who on earth sent them?*

Barbara was eager to get a whiff of her beautiful bouquet, and equally eager to find out who had sent it to her. The possibility of a secret admirer was titillating, and awoke in Barbara the old memory of teenage romance. She tore the clear wrapping off to smell the flowers. As she did, a cloud of white powder popped up from the roses, covering Barbara's nose and mouth. Barbara sneezed as she accidentally inhaled it, and coughed. She quickly found the culprit; the package of rose food had a large tear in it. She examined the label and, determining it was not harmful, threw the offending package in the garbage with the discarded cellophane. There was another envelope of it that she tucked into a drawer in her kitchen.

CHAPTER TWO

Nancy Haskins opened the door, her hands full of mail. Nancy's little Chihuahua, Nelson, immediately jumped on her as she sorted through the bills and put them into the "pay" and "wait" piles on the small table by the entry. Since Burt had passed away, it was all on her now. Electric bill – pay, mortgage bill – pay, water bill – pay, property taxes – wait. No more money. Nancy was 73 years old. She and Burt, who was five years older, had been living under the financial umbrella of social security. But when Burt took ill, Nancy couldn't afford to quit working her regular job as a real estate agent. Retirement for Burt and Nancy was always more of a joke than a dream.

They had begun this dream, as most older couples from the east coast had, with a move to

California to be closer to their daughter, Jillian, and the grandkids. But, after Burt's illness, the bills mounted up and before long that dream had turned into a nightmare.

"Hello, my little Nelson," she said, as she caressed the dog, ruffling his pointed ears and stroking where they connected to his tiny little head, as the last letter slipped onto the floor.

It was from the "Orange Grove Homeowner's Association." Coming from Long Island, a homeowner's association was something foreign to Burt and Nancy, but they had soon learned what it was all about.

"Not again!" Nancy muttered to herself, as Nelson scratched and jumped against her jeans, whining and yelping. Turning her attention to Nelson, she threw the envelope on the "wait" pile.

The nightmare had begun with the color of their house. A year ago, Nancy and Burt received a notice requesting them to paint the exterior of their townhome, which included a detailed list of instructions. They just turned over the instructions to their painter, and asked him to paint the house the same color as the one down the street. It was a pleasant powder blue, and they had always loved it. The painter took a sample from the neighbor's house and matched the color perfectly. The only problem was, unbeknownst to Burt and Nancy, they were not allowed to change the former color of their home. It messed with the "palette" and was a violation of the HOA rules. Nancy and Burt were happy until the HOA sent them a "Notice of Violation," that began a series of legal battles with mounting costs and attorney's fees. It didn't take long for the HOA's fees to pile up higher than a New York City high rise.

Nancy slumped onto the couch and Nelson jumped onto her lap as if he were spring-loaded, and started to play the "biting game." It was his favorite. He charged at Nancy on the couch, and she pushed him away, over and over and over again, and each time, Nelson gently bit at her fingers and growled as he delighted in the attention.

After Nelson calmed down and curled into a tiny ball on the couch, Nancy's mind kept going back to the HOA notice. She and Burt had exhausted all their savings fighting, litigating, and finally settling with them on the paint case after a lengthy mediation. The curiosity nagged at her until she couldn't stand it anymore, although she knew what to expect. Because of the legal bills, mounting expenses, loss of Burt and the economy, the HOA assessments had piled up. Not only that, the Association had added "special assessments" for improvements to the common areas, as well as a ton of attorney's fees. Nancy simply could not afford to pay for them all. She ripped open the envelope to reveal her greatest fear. It read, "Notice of Foreclosure Sale."

CHAPTER THREE

Jean Goldstein had had her share of tragedy in life. Her dream move from New York to California had turned to shit in its third month. Soon after the move, at the age of 16 years, her son, Thomas, lost his life in a car accident. The strain tore apart her marriage, and she and her husband, Gary, stayed together because they couldn't afford to live apart, or maybe just because they didn't know what else to do. Jean had planted a Bigtooth Maple tree in her front yard on the day of her son's funeral in his memory. That was two years ago, and now it had already grown to a healthy height. Jean felt good every time she looked at the tree. Gary had made a wall of stone around the base and affixed a little brass plaque with their son's name on it to the wall.

When the HOA notice had come in only weeks after they had planted the tree, Jean and Gary ignored it. They were from New York and deed restrictions were as foreign to them as a monkey in a suit. After thousands of dollars in legal fees, they had dug in their heels and were now facing potential jail time with a contempt of court citation. It had become a matter of principle to them. Nobody was going to disgrace the memory of their son.

CHAPTER FOUR

By the time Nancy had gathered enough money to hire a lawyer, the foreclosure sale was coming close. Nancy walked into the State Street office of lawyer Brent Marks feeling defeated, but that feeling changed to confidence instantly after he evaluated her case.

Brent looked up from the files and smiled. "It looks to me like they didn't comply with the Davis Stirling Act," Brent told her. "They need to personally serve you with notice of the board's decision to foreclose. This proof of service says they served you by substituted service at your office."

"I'm never at the office. I work out of home."

"That's what substituted service means. If they can't find you at your home or place of business, they can serve an adult there who appears to be in charge. But the Act requires that they personally serve you."

"What do I do?"

"Well, I think it's too late to serve you now, but they may try to do it after we raise the issue. Just be aware."

"I won't answer the front door, and I'll go in and out through the garage by car."

"That will probably work. But, remember, if we win this case, it's just going to delay the inevitable. You'll have to pay the HOA assessments and fees."

"I know. I just need some time."

Time was a precious commodity to Nancy. She needed to close a couple of escrows, and needed to do it fast. In addition to the assessments, there would be legal fees for the HOA and now for her new attorney, Brent Marks.

Brent's secretary, Melinda, an attractive 20 something, brought in the retainer agreement for Nancy to sign. She was what some people may call a "dumb blonde," equipped with stunning blue eyes, but, besides being a little ditzy, she was anything but dumb.

"I'm so happy that I found you, Brent," said Nancy. "I know that you'll put an end to this nightmare."

"It's not going to be easy, Nancy, but I'll do my best."

"I know you will."

Nancy smiled with hope as she signed the agreement, and then reached into her purse for her checkbook.

"This is the best $5,000 I ever spent," she said, as she wrote out the check.

* * *

Back at Orange Grove, Barbara Densmore was staying up late as usual, going over the HOA books. Something about them was just not right. There seemed to be thousands of dollars unaccounted for, and she wanted to prepare as much as she could for her meeting with Frances Templeton, who was also the HOA's treasurer. Barbara had developed a nasty cough over the course of the day, and the cough syrup she had been taking was not helping at all. *I must have caught some kind of flu*, she thought, and it was getting to the point where she felt she needed a doctor. She was achy all over and feverish. As she picked up the phone to call the doctor, it became difficult to breathe and she gasped for breath.

"Call 911 immediately," her physician advised. "I'll meet you at the Cottage Hospital emergency room."

Barbara hung up and did as she was instructed. She was in a panic, her heart was racing, and she was coughing up a white foam, mixed with blood.

Barbara, her body surging with adrenalin, shot up from her seat and headed for the door. The room was spinning as she gasped for air and lost her balance. She reached out to try to catch the top of a chair as she fell to the floor.

CHAPTER FIVE

Barbara Densmore was pronounced dead on arrival at Cottage Hospital. The cause of death was cited as respiratory failure. Barbara's health, in general, had always been good, and her sudden death came as a shock to Dr. Theodore Brown, her regular doctor, who was puzzled, and could not determine what had caused her body to shut down. From the symptoms she exhibited, he suspected it may be some kind of poisoning. He collected samples of the bloody foam discharge, as well as blood and urine samples and sent them to the lab for a toxicology test.

* * *

Frances Templeton knocked on Barbara Densmore's door at precisely 8:30 p.m. for her meeting with Barbara. When Barbara didn't answer, Frances called her cell phone, but it went straight to her voice mail.

"Barbara, are you in there?" called Frances, as she pounded the door.

"Is everything alright?"

Keith Michel, Barbara's next door neighbor, heard the racket, peeled open his non-conforming blue curtain, peered out his window and saw Frances on Barbara's front porch, frantically knocking. *Let the bitch pound on the door until her knuckles bleed,* he thought, and went back to smoking the rest of his roach while he endured his textbook assignment. A part time student and a full time surfer, Keith was one of four guys who roomed together as tenants in the four bedroom townhouse. He hated the HOA just as much as the next guy, no – even more – but the pounding on the door in his hypersensitive state seemed like it was slamming around in his head and reverberating down his spinal cord. He opened the door to put an end to the noise.

"She's not there, Frances."

The surfer. He and his blue curtains have got to go, thought Frances, looking at the super tanned blonde idiot.

"Oh? And how do you know that?"

"The ambulance came for her about an hour ago," said Keith, the wisp of a smile curling from the sides of his chapped lips. Keith didn't like Frances. He didn't like her beady little dark brown eyes. He didn't like her sneaky, faux-feminine mannerisms. And he didn't like her sticking her nose in his business.

"Ambulance?"

"Ask me, she needed a meat wagon."

"Whatever do you mean?"

"She was lifeless, dude. Like a bag o' sand."

"Where did they take her?"

"Who do I look like, 4-1-1?" snickered Keith.

Frances turned her back on Keith without answering and slinked off to her own place, making a mental note to call the HOA attorneys on the rude little addict. Maybe even the police. *Well, maybe not.*

CHAPTER SIX

Dr. Ignacio Perez raised his tired eyes from the microscope, grabbed the stale baloney sandwich from the plate next to the scope and took a bite, with one eye still on the slide.

"Doc, got another live one for ya."

Perez looked up and saw Gabriel Mendez, his assistant, roll in a covered gurney. Mendez was grinning.

"How many times do I have to tell you, Gabriel? This is a place of business. Please respect it."

"I'm not the one eating a sandwich and looking at an HIV sample at the same time," quipped Mendez.

"Gabriel, please!"

"Sorry doc. You got a new stiff."

"Do you think you could stop referring to them as 'stiffs'? These were real people, with real lives."

"Doc, you know me."

"Yeah, yeah, the master of bad jokes."

Gabriel had the annoying habit of trying to make a dumb funny out of every phrase. This didn't make him very popular on the fifth floor, where he used to work, with the aged. The last straw was when Gabriel punned whether he should wheel one of his old senile patients back into his room or down to the morgue. That earned Gabriel a new assignment as assistant to the medical examiner.

Perez stood up, walked over to the body, and peeled back the sheet. He recognized the face right away.

"It's Barbara Densmore," said Perez, as he grabbed the chart at the end of the gurney and flipped through it.

"Who?"

"Barbara Densmore, the head of the Orange Grove Homeowner's Association."

"Huh? An HOA Nazi? No wonder they suspect foul play."

As a resident of Orange Grove, Dr. Perez knew that Densmore was not well liked, but murder?

"Says here that Doctor Brown suspected poisoning. Gabriel, can you please call upstairs for the tox report results?"

"Yeah, sure."

CHAPTER SEVEN

Brent checked and double checked the statute. Civil Code section 1367 clearly said that the decision of the HOA to foreclose had to be made by the HOA's Board, and it had to be personally served on the defendant for the foreclosure to be proper. The case of *Diamond v. Superior Court* required strict compliance with the statute. He would file a complaint for declaratory relief and a motion to enjoin the foreclosure sale.

This was just the type of case that Brent loved. Since he now had the luxury of not having to take any case that walked through the door just to make ends meet, he could concentrate on these David and Goliath cases. Homeowners' Associations gave little people who had little lives a false sense of importance, as well as a real sense of power, over their neighbors. Their boards were almost always composed of people who enjoyed butting into other people's business, and the HOA badge gave them the right to be the neighborhood's policemen. The deed restrictions, or CC&R's as they were known in legal circles, were used by the HOA members to describe a number of serious offenses, such as the wrong color curtains, or an inappropriate and non-conforming landscape. A planned community was definitely no place for anyone to exercise any type of personal freedom over their own property.

Brent's father was an immigrant from Spain. When Brent had taken an ear full of teasing at school because of his last name, Jose Marquez had changed the name to Marks, to avoid the stereotypes that he felt were cast on the family by people who thought they were Mexican. Brent could have passed for Mexican himself, with his dark brown hair, but he was much taller than most Mexicans. Thanks to his dad though, he was fluent in Spanish, which had helped him in the old days when Spanish speaking people made up a majority of his clients.

Although Nancy's case was important, Brent thought that it would be relatively simple. He would file the complaint, make a motion for preliminary injunction, and then refer Nancy to a lender or, if there was no way for her to obtain a loan, to a bankruptcy attorney, to file a chapter 13 plan to take care of the back assessments. The Association also sought foreclosure based on thousands of dollars of attorney's fees they had heaped on top of the assessments. The *Diamond v. Superior Court* case had changed all the foreclosure rules. It was no longer a free for all.

CHAPTER EIGHT

Dr. Perez looked up from the toxicology report, took off his glasses and rubbed his tired eyes. He suspected poisoning from the symptoms Barbara had reported to Dr. Brown but, unfortunately, the report did not reveal the identity of the toxin. From the fluid in her lungs and lesions in the trachea, Perez suspected that it could be ricin, a deadly toxin that produced death relatively quickly and was difficult to detect. Since ricin poisoning was almost never accidental, he called the police immediately. If it was ricin, the best way to identify it was to find the poison at the scene.

* * *

Homicide Detective Roland Tomassi set down the phone and looked at the clock. One hour to go in his shift and he had to go to the morgue and look at another stiff on a slab. *What a job.* He was the last one. *The night shift sucks,* he thought, as he exited the building. *Maybe this will be quick and I can go home early.* Tomassi ruffled his short, sandy brown hair forward with his hands and straightened his old tie, then shut off the lights and closed the door.

Tomassi wandered in to the morgue and saw Dr. Perez exactly as he pictured he would; leaning over a dead body with a sandwich in his hand. Perez looked up at him over the shoulder.

"Hello Detective."

"Hi Doc. What've you got?"

"45 year old female, cause of death suspected is poisoning, but the toxicology report is coming up negative."

Tomassi's forehead wrinkled. "Then why do you suspect poisoning?"

"She was foaming blood right before she died, had an excessive amount of fluid in her lungs, lesions on the trachea and no indication of any other adverse pathology. I suspect it was ricin."

"Ricin?"

"That's why I called you over immediately. You've got to search her home right away to see if you can locate any traces of ricin."

"If that's the case, why didn't you just do this on the phone?"

"Impossible."

"Why not?"

"Because then you wouldn't know the victim."

As they both looked at Barbara's body, the realization of what his job was all about came back to Tomassi.

"To know is to care, right?" he said to the doctor.

"Isn't that why we do what we do?"

Perez was right. The homicide shift was a crappy job, which entailed going to the worst places and seeing the worst things humanity had to offer. But Tomassi had signed on to make a difference. He made a mental note to remember this moment, as he looked at the lifeless, pale face of Barbara Densmore.

"Thanks Doc, for reminding me. Did she have any friends?"

"No, that's it. Everyone hated her."

"Why?"

"She was president of the local homeowners' association."

* * *

When Detective Tomassi pulled his unmarked white Dodge Charger into Barbara Densmore's driveway, he noticed a light in one of the windows.

That's odd, he thought, as he exited the car, and flipped the latch of his holster, putting his left hand on the butt of his service revolver. Tomassi was a leftie, something the guys always teased him about.

As he reached for the doorknob, he was surprised to find it was unlocked. He drew his gun and cautiously entered.

"Police!" he shouted.

"I'm here!" called out the voice of a woman.

Finding the source of the light to be a bedroom, which looked like it doubled as an office, Tomassi gingerly approached the door and instructed the occupant, "Put your hands in the air!" He walked, gun first, into the room.

Frances Templeton did as instructed, shaking nervously as Tomassi slowly approached, with the gun trained on her.

"Now I want you to interlock your fingers behind your head."

Frances complied, in a palsy. Tomassi quickly slapped handcuffs on her and patted her down.

"What's going on?" she asked.

"Who are you? A relative?"

"No, I'm a neighbor. Barbara and I work together. She gave me her key."

"How long have you been here?"

"Just a few minutes. I came to get the books."

"What books?"

"The homeowner's association books. I'm their treasurer and I heard that Barbara was in the hospital. We need the books to prepare for a meeting."

Tomassi unlocked the handcuffs. "Have a seat. A deputy is coming and he will take your information and a statement. I'll take the books for now, and we'll return them in a few days.

"They're on the desk. Am I free to go?"

"Yes, as soon as the deputy is finished taking your statement. Oh, may I have the key please?"

"Of course, but why?"

"This is a crime scene Ms.?"

"Templeton. Frances Templeton. A *crime scene*?"

"Yes, Ms. Templeton. Ms. Densmore died under suspicious circumstances and we have to investigate. I'm sorry for the precautions, but nobody was supposed to be here."

"I understand," said Frances, but the expression on her face could not hide the fact that she was annoyed.

Two deputies arrived, along with the forensics team. The deputies secured the area and took Templeton's statement as the three member forensics team combed the townhome for traces of ricin or any other suspicious chemical agents.

Finally the deputies released Frances. "That's it, ma'am. You're free to go," said Deputy Williams, with a smile, clicking his pen to "off" and slipping it and his book into his pocket.

"Just like that? Without an apology?"

"Ma'am, we're just doing our job."

"And what if I want to file a complaint?"

"You'll need to talk to the Detective for that, ma'am. Our job is finished."

Determined not to let it go, Frances set out to find Tomassi, with the two deputies on her tail.

"Wait a minute, ma'am," said Williams, as he moved in front of her and held out his arm. "This is a crime scene. Stay here with my partner. We'll get him for you."

Tomassi approached Frances with a frown on his face that looked as if he had just taken a bite of a lemon peels .

"What can I do for you, Ms. Templeton?"

"Well, first you can apologize."

"For what?"

"For scaring the wits out of me and treating me like a common criminal."

"Ms. Templeton, do you live here?"

"No, but..."

"Here's how I see it, and feel free to jump in anytime you think I have something wrong. I'm the first officer on a potential homicide scene. The victim lived alone. I park my car, exit and noticed that the lights are on. I approach, enter, and find the residence occupied. For my safety, and the integrity of my investigation, I detain the occupant and, upon determining she is not a threat to my safety, release her from detention and release her completely after questioning her as a potential witness. Do I have it about right?"

"Well yes, but…"

"Then I will continue to do my job, which is to investigate this crime scene. Thank you, Ms. Templeton, you are free to go."

Frances stared into space as if she had been hypnotized, then snapped out of it as Tomassi turned his back on her.

"And if I have a complaint?"

"You're free to make it to my CO, said Tomassi, turning around. Here's my card," he said, holding it out to her. "Call the station and ask for Captain Brooks."

***

The forensic crew worked into the night, sweeping, fingerprinting, and looking for anything that could be used as evidence to explain the mysterious death of Barbara

Densmore. Finally, the team finished, packed up and started to leave.

"We're outta here," said Denny Bingman, the leader of the team.

"What did you get?" asked Tomassi.

"Nothing. Except maybe this package we found in one of the kitchen drawers." Bingman held up a small gold flower food package.

"Flowers? I didn't see any flowers," said Tomassi.

"Neither did we," said Bingman. But you said possible ricin poisoning, so we bagged it."

"Let me know as soon as it's tested."

CHAPTER NINE

Judge Melissa Jones was a fat, pretentious woman, with a healthy dose of attitude for every pound, who had clawed her way to the Santa Barbara County Superior Court bench by proving that she could be just as good a lawyer as any man. The case of *Haskins v. Orange Grove Homeowner's Association* was assigned to her for all purposes, along with the dozens of other cases on her law and motion calendar today. The court had been making budget cuts due to the poor economy, so Jones' courtroom had been understaffed and overworked for the past year and everyone seemed cranky. Still, Brent was optimistic, because Judge Jones was as smart as she was tough, and he had woven a legal web for the Homeowners Association that he thought they could not escape from.

Brent's opponent was Lydia Green, a young woman in her 30's from the firm of Stafford and Green. Her father, Brian Green, had made a fortune milking homeowners associations of a good portion of their monthly dues. Homeowners associations were the best clients for Stafford and Green because they were all run by boards made up of homeowners themselves. Most of the board members were as picky as Barbara Densmore, and didn't mind paying huge fees to enforce the HOA rules. After all, it wasn't their money. Lydia was smartly dressed, in a two piece suit, and had a Chanel briefcase as well as their latest bag. Business was good.

"Number eleven on today's calendar, *Haskins v. Orange Grove Homeowners Association.* Counsel please state your appearances," said Judge Jones into the microphone on her bench.

"Good morning, Your Honor, Brent Marks for the Plaintiff and moving party."

Jones looked down from the bench at Brent through her oversized horn-rimmed glasses.

"Good morning Mr. Marks."

"Good morning, Your Honor, Lydia Green for the Defendant, Orange Grove Homeowner's Association."

"Good morning, Ms. Green. This matter comes on today for a hearing on Nancy Haskins' motion for a preliminary injunction against a foreclosure sale. As you may have noticed, I have not entered a tentative ruling in this case, but I have read the moving papers and the opposition. Mr. Marks, you're the moving party, so I'd like to hear from you first."

"Thank you, Your Honor. In order for a foreclosure sale on an involuntary assessment lien to be valid, the Defendant must not only follow strictly all the provisions of Civil Code 2924, but also the pre-foreclosure procedures in the Davis-Stirling Act, Civil Code Sections 1367.1 and 1367.4, for a foreclosure sale on a delinquent assessment lien to be valid.

"In *Diamond v. Superior Court*, the Court of Appeal ruled that the notice requirements of Sections 1367.1 and 1367.4 must be strictly construed, "pursuant to the plain language of the statutes and their legislative history. Failure to follow these pre-foreclosure requirements makes the foreclosure sale, the Notice of Default and the Notice of Sale null and void.

"In this case, the Defendant's board did not vote to foreclose on the property, as required by the Davis-Stirling Act, until after it had already recorded the Notice of Default. The Code specifies that the decision must be made *before* commencing any foreclosure proceeding. Moreover, they did not personally serve the Plaintiff with the notice of the board's decision to foreclose on the Plaintiff's property, which is required by section 1367.4, serving it instead by substituted service. The *Diamond* case made it perfectly clear that these provisions must be strictly complied with, or any sale will be null and void.

"Both of these are fatal flaws which requires the Court to set aside the sale, and to declare the Notice of Default and Notice of Sale void. Since Mrs. Haskins is about to be put out of title, which will ultimately result in her eviction from her house, she would suffer irreparable injury if the Association were not enjoined from completing the foreclosure before this matter could proceed to trial."

"Thank you, Mr. Marks. Ms. Green?"

Lydia Green stood up from the counsel table to make her argument at the podium. She was skinny, and would have been somewhat attractive had she not chosen to wear a masculine type suit. It looked like she had been in her father's closet, trying on his clothes. Lydia knew that she had better make a convincing argument, because, at this point, if the injunction was granted, the case was virtually over.

"Thank you, Your Honor. First I would like to point out to the Court that Mr. Marks has a conflict of interest in this case. The president of the Association recently died, Your Honor, and, as you can see from the declaration attached to our supplemental papers, the Vice President of the Association, Frances Templeton, has a prior existing attorney client relationship with Mr. Marks."

Brent frowned. He had represented Frances in a divorce some seven years ago. It had nothing to do with the Association.

"Ms. Green, I can't deal with this on today's motion. If you think Mr. Marks is conflicted, then you must raise that issue by a separate motion to disqualify. Now, please address the merits of the motion that *is* before me."

"Thank you, Your Honor. While it is true that the board did not vote on foreclosure until after the Notice of Default was filed, it did vote to foreclose 30 days before filing the Notice of Sale. The statute says that the board vote to approve foreclosure must take place at least 30 days prior to any public sale. The decision being made 30 days before the Notice of Sale, the

Defendant is in compliance with that requirement.

"With regard to the personal service, the statute states that personal service is required in accordance with the manner of service of a summons in Article 3 of Chapter 4 of the Code of Civil Procedure. Substituted service was effected upon Mrs. Haskins at her place of business, in full conformity with Article 3 of Chapter 4. Therefore, the Defendant is in compliance with that requirement.

"Moreover, Your Honor, there is no irreparable injury that the Plaintiff would incur. She owes the assessments, and the Association is entitled to foreclosure to collect them. There is no prejudice to the Plaintiff to wait until a trial of the merits in this case. If she prevails, her remedy is to set aside the sale and quiet title will still be available to her after foreclosure."

"Mr. Marks," asked Judge Jones, "The statute does say the board decision has to be made 30 days before any public sale. Why is the Association's vote not compliant?"

Brent expected this question to arise, so he was prepared.

"Your Honor, the statute plainly says that 'the decision to initiate foreclosure of a lien for delinquent assessments must be made at least 30 days before a public sale. The Association is trying to argue that their board made that decision before initiating foreclosure proceedings, which is also required by the statute, but the recording of a Notice of Default *is* the method of initiating a foreclosure proceeding under Civil Code section 2924, and the Diamond case makes it very clear that the decision must be made before the foreclosure is initiated. When the Association recorded the Notice of Default, it had already initiated foreclosure of the lien. You can't comply with the statute by initiating foreclosure proceedings, then voting to approve the initiation of foreclosure proceedings when they are almost over. The plain meaning of the statute is that it has to be both 30 days before the sale as well as before initiating the proceedings."

"What about the service? The statute says personal service, but it also states that service must be in accordance with the method of serving summons in Article 3. Doesn't that include substituted service?"

Brent didn't like the direction the Judge seemed to be moving in. He thought she was smarter than that. Perhaps she was just making a record in case she was appealed.

"Your Honor, the plain meaning of the statute, which the *Diamond* case says must be followed strictly, is that *personal* service is required. It states, 'The board shall provide notice by personal service in accordance with the manner of service of summons in Article 3.' Article 3 spells out the requirements for both personal service and substituted service. They are two separate types of service, and the statute clearly calls for *personal* service. Substituted service is not strict compliance with the statutory requirements because the plain meaning of the statute specifies personal service in accordance with Article 3 as *the only method of service.*

"This is supported by the legislative intent behind the statute. The legislative history of the sections is set forth in the Legislative Counsel's Digest, which are cited in my brief. According to that legislative history of the bill and the plain meaning of the statute itself, personal service of notice of the decision to foreclose upon the owner/occupier is required as a condition of the right to foreclose. Without that personal service, the foreclosure right does not arise, no matter what."

"Ms. Green, do you wish to be heard?"

"Yes, Your Honor. The statute is clearly ambiguous. It is obviously not the best written statute. It specifies that service by made pursuant to Article 3, and substituted service is one of the methods to effect personal service under Article 3. The Association is in complete compliance."

"Thank you, Ms. Green."

"Your Honor, may I be heard please on this point?"

"Of course, Mr. Marks."

"Personal service is not effected by substituted service. They are two separate kinds of service specified in Article 3, and the statute clearly requires personal service. If you look at the legislative history, you will see that these protections were put into the Davis-Stirling Act to prohibit a homeowners' association from taking a resident's property for a relatively small assessment bill. The legislature clearly intended foreclosure to be a method to force the collection of delinquent assessments, not to dispossess residents of their property.

"The reason for the personal service to be in accordance with Article 3, Section 415.10 is to give notice of a legal process in order to comply with the principles of due process. The Fourteenth Amendment to the United States Constitution provides that 'no state shall deprive any person of life, liberty or property without due process of law.' The legislative history of the amendment creating Section 1367.4, plainly requires the HOA board to provide personal service to an owner/occupant of its decision to foreclose as a condition of foreclosure, which is a taking of property authorized by the state. Notice is a concept of due process, and since it required that notice to be given by personal service, as opposed to the other methods of service specified in the Code of Civil Procedure, the Legislature plainly prescribed the highest form of notice.

"The purpose of such service statutes is to assure that the highest form of due process is satisfied. Clearly, since the statute specifies personal service of the board's decision is a precondition of foreclosure, the notice must be personally served before the commencement of any foreclosure proceedings, to allow the homeowner notice and the opportunity to defend against them."

"Thank you both. The matter being submitted, I am ready to rule. I think the statute clearly says that the decision to foreclose has to be made 30 days before any public sale, and this was done."

Brent was immediately deflated. He had lost, and Nancy would have to take her chances with the Bankruptcy Court.

"But," continued Judge Jones, "I think that the statute clearly requires personal service of the notice of the board's decision – not substituted service – so I am going to grant the motion for a preliminary injunction against foreclosure pending the trial on this matter."

"Thank you, Your Honor," said Brent, relieved.

"Thank you, Your Honor," said the defeated Lydia Green.

Brent headed out of the courtroom, activating his cell phone to call Nancy and tell her the good news.

CHAPTER TEN

While Brent was celebrating his victory with Nancy, Detective Roland Tomassi was making the rounds, questioning each of Barbara Densmore's neighbors. None of them had any kind words for Barbara. As he thumbed through his notes, an old VW van with a surfboard on top of it pulled into the driveway next door to Barbara's townhome. As Tomassi approached the driver, a long haired blond man wearing flower patterned baggies and no shirt exited the car and began untying his surfboard from the roof rack.

"Hello!" called out Tomassi, as he approached.

"Sup dude?" Keith Michel greeted him.

"I'm a police detective. Name's Detective Tomassi. Do you mind if I ask you a few questions about your neighbor, Barbara Densmore?"

"It's a free country," responded Keith Michel. "Did she croak?"

"Why do you ask?"

"Dude, she didn't look like she was in too good 'a shape when they took her out in the ambulance."

"You saw them take her out?"

"Yeah."

"You don't seem to be too concerned about her."

"Dude, she's a pain in my ass. She's a pain in everyone's ass. Well, if you live here, that is…"

"I'm investigating her death."

"Oh, so she did croak? Righteous!"

"You're happy that she's dead?"

"Dude, I didn't kill her or anything, but I'm not gonna cry either. She was always so aggro, you know?"

"Aggro?"

"Yeah, you know, not cool, always messin' with my vibe. Whenever I was all stoked and amped to go out, she'd come over and write me a ticket or some shit. She was a downer, man."

"I see. Can you tell me how long you had been at home before you saw the ambulance come for her?"

"I dunno. Man, I don't have a time clock or anything."

"Rough estimate."

"Man, I guess two, three hours?"

"Did you notice anything unusual over at her place during those two or three hours?"

"Dude, I don't snoop on her or nothin'. I was just lookin' out the window and saw the ambulance, is all. Oh, and I saw Frances Templeton, the other HOA Nazi, over there banging on Barbara's door."

"Was that the only time that day you saw Frances over there?"

"Yeah."

"And when was that?"

"Dude!"

"Were you having any problems with Ms. Densmore?"

"Just the usual stuff. She didn't like my curtains. You know, shit like that."

"Yeah. Do you mind if I come in and take a look around?"

"Dude, you got a warrant? Knock yourself out."

"How about if I take a look in your car instead? I'll bet I could find some marijuana in there."

"Dude, I've got a scrip for that, uh, for my medical condition."

"I'll bet you do. What's your name?"

"Keith Michel."

"Alright, Mr. Michel, here's my card. In case you think of anything else, just give me a call."

"Thanks, dude," said Michel, taking the card. "I'll be sure to file this in the appropriate place," he added, smiling an ear to ear mouthful of yellow teeth.

As Tomassi turned away, Michel added, "Might want to check out the couple at 4440 Orange. They hated Barbara's guts."

"Thanks, I will."

* * *

At 4440 Orange, Jean Goldstein looked through the peep hole on her front door.

"Can I help you?" she asked through the door.

"My name is Roland Tomassi, Detective with the Santa Barbara County Sheriff."

Jean opened the door. "How can I help you, Detective?"

"I'd like to ask a few questions about Barbara Densmore."

"What's she done this time?"

"She died."

Goldstein frowned.

"Died?"

"Yes, ma'am. I'm investigating her death."

"I hope you don't think we had anything to do with it?"

"Just talking to the neighbors, ma'am. May I come in?"

"Of course."

Jean led Detective Tomassi into her living room.

"Can I offer you a drink, Detective?"

"No, thank you."

Detective Tomassi sat down on the couch in the hodge-podge of a living room, filled with family photographs of different sizes and shapes, and pulled out his notebook. Jean was in her late 40's, with greying chestnut hair and amber eyes. Tomassi could see that, in her day, she must have been quite attractive, but, to him, she mostly looked sad.

"I understand you're currently in litigation with the Homeowners' Association?"

"Yes. Over the most ridiculous thing. A tree."

"A tree?"

"My husband and I planted a Big Tooth Maple in the front yard to honor the life of our son, Thomas."

"Thomas is deceased?"

Jean's lip quivered. "At sixteen. We lost him in a tragic accident." Her eyes welled up with tears.

"That him?" Tomassi asked, pointing to a picture of a young boy in a silver frame on the coffee table. Jean nodded, and wiped the tears from her eyes with her fingers.

"I'm sorry for your loss, ma'am."

"Thank you, Detective. I don't think it's something that anyone can get used to, no matter how much time passes."

"I suppose not, ma'am. I can't imagine losing a child."

"We never thought...Anyway, Barbara gave us a ticket to take down the tree because we didn't go through the landscape committee for pre-approval."

"And you didn't want to remove the tree."

"Of course not. But Barbara wouldn't let it go. Her rules are so – *were* – so important to her."

"Ma'am, do you mind if I take a look around?"

"Am I under arrest?"

"No, nothing like that. Just asking your permission for a voluntary search."

"Sure, go ahead. I have nothing to hide."

"Thank you, ma'am."

CHAPTER ELEVEN

Tomassi was exhausted. After every interview, he turned up a new possible suspect. It seemed that Barbara Densmore was more hated in Orange Grove than Osama bin Laden. Tomassi couldn't arrest every resident in Orange Grove. He had to retrace his steps. Gathering his field deputy's notes, he decided to pay a visit to Frances Templeton. Templeton had called the station, not to complain, but to report that she had a lead.

"Detective. Did you come to apologize?"

"No ma'am. Just to go over a few details on your lead, if you have the time."

"Well alright, come in then."

Frances must have been the type of person for whom everything had to be in order. Her house was so neat, it appeared that nobody lived there. *Typical control freak,* thought Tomassi.

"How can I help you, Detective?"

"You told Deputy Williams that Barbara had words with one of the residents. A Nancy..."

"Haskins."

"Yes, Nancy Haskins. What exactly did you see, Ms. Templeton?"

"Well, Barbara was making her usual rounds."

"Rounds?"

"Yes, enforcement rounds. We both do them; you know, looking for violators."

"You're talking about a neighborhood watch program?"

"Goodness no, we have that too, but I'm talking about Code violations."

"Code violations, ma'am?"

"You know. Violations of the regulations of the Homeowners' Association. We have to protect our property values, you know?"

"I see. So Barbara was making her rounds, and?"

"She was aggressed by Haskins. Barbara tried to give her a citation for an overgrown lawn and Haskins ran into her house, yelling 'shove your ticket up your…' well, you know…and she gave her the finger!"

"That's hardly a motive for murder, ma'am. In fact, as I understand it, Ms. Densmore was not a very loved personality in the neighborhood."

"You just go talk to her. You'll see."

"I will ma'am, thank you."

* * *

When Tomassi arrived at the home of Nancy Haskins, he knocked on the door and was about to give up, when he heard a voice from inside, along with the sounds of a little dog yapping.

"Who is it?"

"Detective Roland Tomassi, Santa Barbara County Sheriff."

"Show me your badge, please."

Tomassi pulled out his wallet and held the badge in front of the peep hole. The door opened, and there stood a woman who looked to be in her 70's who could have passed for Tomassi's mother, with a little Chihuahua jumping and scratching at her pants.

"Ms. Haskins?"

"Mrs. Haskins. You can call me Nancy. Would you care to come in?" she asked, with a pleasant smile, and stood aside.

"Thank you."

Once inside, Tomassi scanned the townhome. It seemed comfortable and homey. He expected Nancy to offer him some home-baked cookies.

"Would you like to sit down, Officer?"

"It's Detective, actually. Thank you," he said, taking a seat in one of the two old fashioned cushy arm chairs. Nancy took a seat on the couch across from him. "I'm investigating the death of one of your neighbors, Barbara Densmore."

"I heard about that."

Nancy did not appear to show any remorse at all, but maybe that had been her initial reaction when she had heard the news. Then again, Tomassi had not been met with heartfelt sympathy from any of the neighbors he had interviewed.

"Can I get you something? Maybe some tea or coffee?"

Here come the cookies. "No thanks, ma'am. I won't be long."

"I understand the Homeowners' Association is foreclosing on your house."

"Yes, but they actually suffered a major setback two days ago, when we won against them in court."

"I see. One of your neighbors, Frances Templeton, said you had words with Barbara not too long ago. Can you tell me about that?"

"Frances, huh? She could be Barbara's twin. Am I a suspect or something?"

"No ma'am, this is just a routine interview."

"I see. Okay. I don't know what you call it, but I was constantly hiding from Barbara's process servers, so when she called to me as I was going inside my house, I ran inside quickly because I thought it may be a trick."

"I see. And do you remember what you said to her?"

"Not really. She was trying to give me another one of her tickets. She writes them to everyone, and I wasn't interested in it. I have a whole collection of them."

Tomassi talked with Nancy for a while, and felt relatively comfortable in scratching her off the suspect list. Still, he took a shot at a routine search, like he had done with the others.

"Do you mind if I look around, ma'am?"

"I thought I wasn't a suspect. Am I being arrested?"

"You're definitely not, ma'am. I just need to cover all the bases with every interview."

"I don't need a lawyer, do I?"

"Ma'am, it's your right to call your lawyer, but, just between you and me, I don't think you need to."

"And the others agreed?"

"Some did, some didn't. It's completely voluntary."

"Well, I suppose, but you're not going to find anything."

"Thank you, ma'am."

* * *

Tomassi actually felt guilty looking through the lady's house, so he made it a quick, cursory search.

"Just have to look in the garage, and then I'll be done," he said to Nancy, as he opened the door to the garage.

"It's just a garage."

Tomassi entered the garage and turned on the light. He looked around quickly, and started to leave, but out of the corner of his eye, he noticed the light glinting off some crumpled glossy plastic which was sticking out of one of the trash cans. He pulled out his handkerchief and examined it, and noticed it was covered with a grayish white powder. He also noticed a gold package of flower food that had been ripped open. He carefully put all of it in an evidence bag, and left the garage.

"What's that?" asked Nancy.

"I found it in your garage, in the garbage. Do you have any fresh flowers in the house?"

"No. And I've never seen that plastic wrap before. It was in my garbage?"

"Yes ma'am. Do you always leave your garage side door unlocked, ma'am?"

"I've been forgetting to lock it lately since I won the case. I guess I let my guard down. Do I need a lawyer?"

"That's up to you, ma'am. As I said, I'm not arresting you, but I still have to get this analyzed."

"Oh, my!"

Nancy frowned, and put her hand on her forehead. Tomassi felt bad, but he was a detective first, and this was his only lead. He would have the lab analyze it right away and it should clear the matter up.

CHAPTER TWELVE

Brent was still high from the court victory when he got the call from Nancy.

"Slow down Nancy…what?"

"They think I murdered Barbara Densmore."

"Where are you?"

"I'm home. The Detective just left. He searched my house…"

"Did he ask permission?"

"Yes."

"And you agreed?" asked Brent, raising his voice.

"Of course, Brent. I had nothing to do with Barbara's death."

"Unfortunately Nancy, it doesn't ever really matter what the truth is. Only what they think it is. Now take a deep breath and let's go over this step by step."

Brent knew that anyone could be convicted of anything. It didn't really matter if you were guilty or not. If they decided to pin it on you – you were guilty – period. After Nancy unloaded her story, she felt better, and agreed not to talk to anyone unless she talked to Brent first.

Brent closed up the office and said good bye to his secretary, Melinda.

"Going to see your favorite FBI agent, boss?" she asked, her blue eyes sparkling.

"Now, how did you know?"

"It's my psychic powers. Now don't you think I deserve a raise?"

"A what? Ahem!" said Brent, clearing his throat.

"See you tomorrow, boss," she said to Brent as he walked out the door.

* * *

Angela Wollard was waiting for Brent at their usual table at the El Paseo restaurant. She reached into her purse, pulled out her pocket mirror and looked at herself quickly. As an FBI agent, looking feminine was not on the top of her list, but as Brent Mark's girlfriend, she couldn't just rely on her natural five foot eight inch curvy frame and green eyes. She had to make sure she always looked good for him. Brent arrived just as Angela was switching the mirror for her cell phone, and checking her email.

"Always at work, aren't you Agent Wollard?"

Brent put his hand on Angela's shoulder and leaned over to kiss her.

"You think I am, but I was just waiting for you."

Before long, they were sipping on margaritas (Angela's was a virgin) and swapping work stories.

"It looks like I may be getting a capital case," said Brent.

"I thought you didn't take criminal cases anymore."

"It's for my HOA client."

"The one whose house you saved from foreclosure?"

"Yeah, Nancy Haskins. She's suspected of killing the HOA president."

"Murder?'

'Well she certainly had a motive. They searched her house today and left with some evidence. Detective Tomassi from the Sherriff's Department."

"I know Tomassi. He's a good cop."

"Yeah – good enough to search a house without a warrant."

"Did she consent?"

"Apparently so."

"Then?" asked Angela.

"Then, what's the problem, right?"

"Whether she's guilty or not."

"Very good! Now, you're thinking like a lawyer instead of just a cop."

"And you expect to be able to think like a lawyer too, going back to the office after two margaritas?"

"Charles Stinson and I used to have martini lunches and then go back to the office."

"What could you possibly do at the office after a martini lunch?"

"For Charles, it was having another martini. If you popped the head off the eagle statue on his desk, you would discover it was full of vodka."

* * *

After the lunch hour at the Santa Barbara Sheriff's office, it was not so relaxed. The tests had come back from the lab on the cellophane wrap and flower food package positive for ricin and with Barbara Densmore's fingerprints all over them. Tomassi reached for the phone and called the Medical Examiner.

"Dr. Perez, we got the tests back on evidence found in the Densmore case. You were right, it was ricin poisoning."

"I knew it. How was it delivered?"

"Flowers. We figure when she opened the plastic wrapping, a packet of what looked like flower food was full of ricin and it was rigged to pop open."

"So she inhaled the ricin."

"That's what we think."

"And it's consistent with my findings of lesions in the trachea. Just as well, I'm going to conduct a further examination."

"Let me know what you come up with, Doc."

Tomassi hung up the phone and called his deputies to action.

"Clark, find out what flower store sold these flowers and who ordered them."

"Will do."

"Williams, let's prepare an affidavit for an arrest warrant on Haskins."

CHAPTER THIRTEEN

By the time Brent had sobered up, it was time to go home and feed the cat. After that, a quick shower and then off to Angela's for what would promise to be another wonderful evening. As Brent descended Harbor Hills Drive, the sun was playing a fantastic game of spectrum as it tucked itself beneath the horizon. Angela's apartment was great, but Brent thought that, if they ever did live together, it should be here. Nothing was better than kicking back on the balcony in the fresh air and that fantastic harbor view, at any time of day or night.

Brent almost tripped over Calico as she slinked between his ankles, purring and mewing. Calico won the race to the kitchen, and Brent couldn't pour the kibble out fast enough. She promptly forgot about him as she buried her purring face in her bowl and crunched away.

* * *

Just as Brent was getting out of the shower, the phone rang. How he hated the phone, especially after being on it all day at the office. He wrapped a towel around himself and dripped over to it to answer.

"Hello?"

"Boss, it's Melinda. I have an emergency call for you from Nancy Haskins. Can I put her through?"

"Sure, go ahead."

Lawyers are not doctors, and there are not many legal emergencies that can't wait until the next day. Still, Brent knew that the cops had given Nancy a hard time that day. Nancy's voice came in spurts.

"Brent, I've been arrested! What do I do?"

"Nancy, calm down. The first thing we need to do is get you out of there, but you may have to spend the night in jail."

"In jail! How could this happen? I didn't kill anybody! I couldn't!"

"I'm going to help you, Nancy, but none of this is going to be cheap. You'll need money for a bail bond, for starters. Can you borrow money from anyone?"

"I don't know. I suppose so."

"Good. Think of everyone who can possibly help you with money. I'm going to put you back with Melinda and she'll call the bondsmen and your potential lenders for you and find out when your court date is. I'll be there for you, so don't worry. Take a deep breath, slow down and calmly give her as much information as you can."

* * *

Judge Burt Hendron's courtroom was a masterpiece of 1927 Santa Barbara architecture. It had leather covered wooden pews for gallery seats and the walls were plastered with murals depicting the discovery of California and the establishment of the missions by Father Junipero Serra. The defendants in custody were escorted into the jury box by the Sheriff's deputies. All wore blue jail jumpsuits and ankle chains, including one shivering Nancy Haskins.

Brent asked permission to speak to Nancy, and went over to remind her of everything they had gone over on the phone. This was an arraignment, where she would plead not guilty and then Brent would ask for her to be released on her own recognizance, without bail. If that was refused, he would ask for a small amount of bail to be set, and the judge would set the matter for a preliminary hearing.

The clerk called the courtroom to order and Judge Hendron took the bench. After about a half hour of pouring through his calendar, he finally called Nancy's case.

"The People of the State of California versus Nancy Haskins, case number C1224356. Counsel please state your appearances."

"Deputy District Attorney Sandra Field for the People, Your Honor."

"Good morning, Ms. Field."

"Brent Marks for the Defendant, Your Honor."

"Good morning, Mr. Marks. This case is on today for arraignment."

Nancy stood up as Brent had previously instructed.

"Yes, Your Honor. The Defendant is present and represented by counsel and waives further reading of rights and charges," said Brent.

"Very well, Mr. Marks. Mrs. Haskins, to the charge of murder in the first degree, how do you plead?"

"Not guilty, Your Honor."

"Your plea of not guilty is taken. Before I set a preliminary hearing, I would like to hear from counsel on the matter of bail."

"Your Honor, the Defendant moves that she be released on her own recognizance. She is a member of the local community for more than 15 years, and is gainfully employed here as well, and bears no flight risk."

Judge Hendron eyeballed Brent from the top of his wire rimmed glasses. "A member of the community who is accused of murdering her neighbor, Mr. Marks."

Field took the cue from the judge and chimed in. She had a shopping cart full of files and the arraignment was about as far as she would see any of these cases go. But she had read every one of the files and was prepared to argue bail.

"This is a capital case, Your Honor. The People request bail in the amount of $1 million."

"Mr. Marks?" asked Judge Hendron.

"That is tantamount to a denial of bail, Your Honor. The Defendant cannot afford to post a million dollar bail. If the Court insists on bail, it should be set at something the Defendant can bond."

"What do you suggest, Mr. Marks?"

"Fifty Thousand Dollars, Your Honor."

"Your Honor, Fifty Thousand Dollars is outrageous for a capital case. Physical evidence of the murder weapon was found on the Defendant's property. This was a pre-meditated act." said Field.

"Your Honor, the only thing tying the evidence that Ms. Field is talking about to the Defendant is that it was found in her garbage. It didn't have any of her fingerprints on it, Your Honor, and it was plastic wrapping for flowers but no flowers were ever found. It could have easily been planted there."

"Save the arguments for trial. Bail is set at One Hundred Thousand Dollars," said Hendron. "Does your client waive time for preliminary hearing and trial?"

Brent knew that, since he had set aside the foreclosure sale and the title to Nancy's townhome was clear, his bail bondsman would write a bond secured by her home for $100,000.

"Yes, Your Honor."

CHAPTER FOURTEEN

Back at the office, Brent had an appointment with his investigator, Jack Ruder. Jack was a 50-something ex-FBI agent from L.A. who was living his dream retirement in Santa Barbara. Jack walked into Brent's office wearing a grey G-Man type suit. Lean, fit and looking ten years younger than his age, he could have been on the cover of an FBI training manual

"Hey, Jack. Damn it if you don't always look like a cop."

"What're you talking about?"

"Nothing Jack. Sit down, we've got a lot to cover. Now, I've talked to all of the potential witnesses just to feel them out, you know, but you're going to have to get in there and talk to them like a cop."

"I think I may be able to do that, Brent."

"I thought so. Be careful of that Keith Michel. He's a wiseass."

"Should I also talk to Mrs. Haskins?"

"Especially her, Jack. I'd like to know if we're defending an innocent woman or not."

"What do you think?" asked Jack, furrowing his brow and leaning in toward Brent.

"Why, Jack, it looks like you really care."

"Of course I do."

"I see the Boy Scout has never grown up. Me too, Jack. I care whether our client is guilty or not and I just don't buy it. Plus, I believe the old lady. I think someone set her up."

* * *

Jack's first stop on his tour was Detective Roland Tomassi's office.

"Hey, Jack, been a while," said Tomassi when Jack popped his head into his office.

"Got a minute?"

"Yeah, come on in."

Jack sat down in one of the two steel chairs in front of Tomassi's not so impressive desk, stacked with papers, files and pictures of his wife and kids.

"I'm on the Haskins case," said Jack.

"What can I do for you, Jack? All the discovery has to go through the D.A."

"I know. We've got the initial discovery. I've looked at the evidence and the reports, and I just don't get something."

"What?"

"Why would the perp rig the ricin to pop off in the victim's face, and then come back to erase all the evidence, but take the flower wrapping home to throw it away?"

"I asked myself the same thing."

"And where are the flowers?"

"We never found them."

"It just doesn't make sense, Rolly. I think you've arrested the wrong person."

"It's what we've got. The evidence is telling us what happened, Jack, not the other way around. Evidence doesn't lie."

"I know, but it doesn't make sense."

"In our world does anything really make sense?"

* * *

Jack's rounds with the neighbors were not popping up any new leads either, except for the fact that, whomever he listened to, the person he interviewed seemed to reveal a new possible suspect. There was the pot smoking surfer who made no bones about the fact that he was glad Barbara was dead, the couple with the dead son who didn't feel the slightest bit of remorse about her passing; almost all of the residents in Orange Grove seemed to be happier now that Barbara was gone.

Jack finished his neighborhood tour just as it was getting dark. He decided to top off the day with a visit to Frances Templeton, who grudgingly admitted him into her home.

"I don't have a lot of time, Mr. Ruder."

"That's alright ma'am, neither do I."

Templeton showed Jack in, but remained standing with her hands on her hips and didn't offer him a seat.

"Brent Marks has already talked to me."

"I know."

"Did you also know that Brent represented me in my divorce?" she asked, coldly.

"Yes ma'am, I do. Do you think that this fact compromises his representation of Mrs. Haskins?"

"Well it surely does as far as the Association is concerned," Templeton huffed.

"I don't see that it's relevant in a murder case."

"Well, ask what you're going to ask. I've got about five minutes."

"Did you ever witness Mrs. Haskins to threaten Ms. Densmore in any way?"

"Like I told the detective, she practically attacked Barbara when she just tried to give her a citation."

"You mean when she told Barbara to shove the ticket and gave her the finger?"

"Yes!"

"Did she threaten her life in any way?"

"She was violent!"

"What did she do besides tell Barbara to shove the ticket and show her finger?"

"Well, she…"

"Nothing else?"

"Well, no, but…"

"And you never saw anything else that could be considered a violent threat to Barbara?"

"Well, there was the time she threatened to kill both of us."

"She threatened to kill you?"

"Yes, she did."

"How was that?"

"We had just served her with a notice of default to foreclose on her house…"

"Yes?"

"And she was driving by Barbara's house. We were standing outside and she yelled from the car, 'I wish you both were dead!'"

"I see. That's exactly what she said?" asked Jack, taking notes.

"Yes, she said she wished we both were dead. And now Barbara is dead, and if you get that woman out of jail, I may be next."

* * *

As Jack was leaving the rather uneventful interview with Frances Templeton, he noticed a bright light next door. It seemed to be seeping from a crack in the weather-stripping around the garage. Since he needed to talk to Keith Michel anyway, he walked toward the light onto the driveway, and noticed that the side door to the garage was ajar.

"Mr. Michel?" he called, as he pushed the door open wider.

Jack felt a jab in his gut from the dark and looked forward to find the barrel of a shotgun shoved against his abdomen.

"Make a move and I blow you away!"

CHAPTER FIFTEEN

Jack froze, as a surge of adrenalin brought the hairs on his neck to full alert and beads of sweat instantly popped out on his forehead.

"Hands up!" said the stranger with the shotgun. He was Hispanic, around his mid-30's and wearing surfer gear; probably one of Michel's roommates. Jack immediately complied.

"You got a warrant, Chupas?"

"I'm not a cop. I'm a private investigator."

"You look like a cop."

"Everyone says that," ventured a smiling Jack, his half-assed attempt at humor to lighten the situation.

"What are you doing here, cabron?"

"I came to talk to Keith Michel."

"Why don't you use the front door like everyone else? I could've blown you away." The fat stranger patted Jack down with his left hand, keeping the shotgun pinned against his gut, and removed Jack's Glock 9mm from his shoulder holster. "And you're packin." The stranger tucked the gun into his pocket. "Looks like we got us a situation," he said, taking a couple of paces backward.

"Can I just come in and explain?"

"You ain't explainin nothin."

"Could you at least put the shotgun down? I'm not armed anymore."

The stranger put the shotgun at his side and Jack exhaled nervously, but not loud enough so that the stranger could notice. This business required a thick skin of discipline. Jack recalled the day when, as an LAPD cop before his FBI days, he answered a domestic violence call. One moment, the woman had been standing in front of him in the doorway, animated and ranting and raving about her husband and the next moment she was gone and in her place was a man holding a smoking shotgun with a blank look on his face. Inside, Jack was crumbling apart, but on the outside, he appeared to have nerves of steel when he commanded the man to turn over the gun.

Jack averted his eyes over the stranger's shoulder to try to get a look into the garage.

"Whaddaya lookin at?" yelled the stranger, going for the shotgun.

"Nothing, nothing. Look, just give me my gun back and I'll leave."

The stranger took the Glock out of his pocket, ejected the clip, slid open the slide and checked the chamber, then emptied out the clip, popping bullets onto the pavement, and slammed the slide back with the precision of a knowledgeable gun handler. He handed the gun back to Jack, and immediately took up his shotgun again, standing at ready position.

"Can you please tell Mr. Michel to give me a call?"

"Whadda I look like? An answering service?"

"I'll give you my card, may I?" Jack asked, reaching for his vest pocket, and resisting the urge to answer the stranger's question. The stranger nodded and waved the shotgun. Jack took out the card and handed it to him.

* * *

While Jack was on his field trip, Brent was enjoying some well-deserved rest and relaxation, with no clients and no cats. He had gone home after leaving the office to feed the cat, shower and freshen up for his date with Angela. When he arrived to her two-level Spanish style apartment, he practically ran past the fountains and gardens which usually gave him pause because they were so beautiful. It was true that being apart built up anticipation, but it was beginning to be a real killer.

Brent knocked on the door of Angela's apartment, and she opened it, wearing hardly anything but a smile.

"Quick, come in," she said, as she pulled him inside.

"Oh, I get it. You're getting ready, uh, where do you want to go?"

"Brent are you blind?" said the light-haired green eyed beauty in the slinky blue silk bathrobe that barely covered her small round bottom.

"Huh?"

Angela knew that once Brent "got it," all the time she spent on preparation would be appreciated. *Sometimes men are so dense,* she thought. She leaned forward for a kiss so Brent could not quite embrace her, but could get a good whiff of her scent.

"We're staying here tonight."

Brent tried to softly pull her to him for a hug, but she broke away, giggling.

"I'm making you dinner," she said, pulling the tie on her robe and letting it fall to the ground, exposing lacy negligee that barely covered her small but perfectly rounded breasts, and left not a lot to the imagination. "And I'm dessert."

CHAPTER SIXTEEN

Jack Ruder was on time, as usual, but not as crisp as he normally appeared, when he walked into Brent's office.

"Long night, Jack?" asked Brent.

"Long and hard."

"Sounds like the title of a porno movie."

"Very funny," said Jack, as he sat down in the wooden chair in front of Brent's desk with a sigh. "Can't you afford a more comfortable chair?"

"Dude, those cost me a fortune. Besides, we don't want clients to get too comfortable. Just long enough to say what's necessary."

"I thought you charged by the hour."

"Well, Jack, since you do too, let's get down to it. What've you got so far?"

"Well, first of all I was almost shot by a Hispanic guy with a shotgun."

"Really?" Brent at once felt out of his joking mood.

"Keith Michel's house. As I was leaving my interview with Frances Templeton, I noticed the garage side door was ajar at Michel's house. I needed to talk to him anyway, so I approached. Before I knew it, I was cozying up to a shotgun. Almost pissed my pants."

"What do you make of it?"

"I think it has something to do with drugs. Maybe a meth lab. Tomassi says Michel's a pothead. Maybe they're growing marijuana."

"Interesting that a meth lab might be right next door to Templeton and all she can think about is blue curtains."

"Yeah, but I don't think it's the greatest lead for us."

"Instincts aside, Jack, we're dealing with creating reasonable doubt here. If Barbara Densmore got too snoopy and discovered something she shouldn't have seen, that's a great motive for the killer to take her out. Let's pursue it."

"Even if it turns into an agency or a DEA case?"

"Especially if it does. What about the couple with the dead son?"

"I'm not wild about that lead, either. The wife is pretty likeable."

"Some of the most likeable people on the outside are capable of truly heinous things."

"I know. I'll keep following that one. I still haven't talked to the husband. There's a lot of people who live in Orange Grove who weren't sad to see Densmore go. But they don't like Templeton either."

"How did it go with her?"

"Got nothing out of that one."

"But don't let it go."

"Roger that."

"Anything else?"

"That's about it. It's going to take some time Brent. Do you need any of this for the preliminary hearing?"

"No. This is going to trial no matter what. The prelim is just for going through the motions. We know the judge will hold Nancy to answer. Just let me have your notes from your interviews with Detective Tomassi. It might help with the suppression motion."

"Right."

* * *

Nelson sat by the table while Nancy ate her lunch, intently staring at every move she made, with the cutest look he could manage on his face. Nancy picked at her food. She hadn't had an appetite since getting out of jail. She looked at Nelson and smiled. She could never get over how cute he was.

"Don't worry, baby. Mommy hasn't forgotten about you."

Now that Burt was gone, Nelson was the only friend that Nancy had, and who knows for how long. *Well,* she thought, *You could say that about anyone.* We are all alone in this world; even in a crowd.

Nancy picked up her almost full plate and headed to the kitchen, with Nelson jumping at her heels. She selected a small piece of chicken to give him, and he was already twirling in circles and going through his whole repertoire of tricks to earn it.

"This is going to be easy today, Nelson," she said as she dropped the piece of chicken. Nelson caught it and continued his floor show. Nancy couldn't hang around for more. She had an important meeting with Brent Marks.

* * *

Brent was just finishing his lunch with Angela at a quaint little café right across from the Santa Barbara courthouse. Santa Barbara was a small town, but it had over 100 restaurants. They sat at a table on the patio, where they could enjoy the view of the beautiful courthouse gardens.

"Your preliminary hearing is tomorrow, isn't it?" asked Angela.

"Yes, it is."

"How does it look?"

"In state court, it's pretty basic. We know that the judge is going to hold Nancy to answer.

The only question is: how will he rule on the motion to suppress."

"They don't get granted too often, do they?"

"No, and Detective Tomassi is going to say she gave her consent for the search."

"Then why make the motion?"

"I'm not so sure she knew what she was consenting to. Anyway, she's coming into the office in about 15 minutes, so I have to run."

* * *

When Brent got back to the office, Nancy was already there in the waiting room, fidgeting in her chair.

"Hi Nancy, I'll be right with you. Any messages Mimi?" Brent asked his secretary.

"No, it's been pretty quiet here."

"Thanks. Okay Nancy, come on in."

Brent led Nancy to his office and she sat down.

"Brent I'm so nervous," she said, as she took off her round horn-rimmed glasses to clean them.

"Don't worry Nancy. As I told you before, this is just a preliminary hearing. It's to determine if the judge thinks they have enough evidence to hold a trial, and I can guarantee you that in almost 100% of all cases, he does. All he has to do is find probable cause to hold you over. There's nothing we can do to avoid a trial."

"That's not reassuring, Brent, but I trust you," Nancy said, her hands shaking.

"And I'm not calling you to testify. There's no point to tell your story now."

"Why not?"

"Because, first, you have a right not to say anything. And second, it won't help you no matter what you say at this point. Like I said, this is going to trial and if you tell your story, you'll tell it to the jury because they're the ones who will be making the decision. The only thing that could keep this from going to trial is a favorable ruling on our motion to suppress."

"What are the chances of winning that?"

"Slim to none, but it may help us later if we have to appeal."

"Appeal?" Nancy's forehead wrinkled, her eyes wide with fear.

"Let's do this with baby steps, Nancy. First, let's get through the motion to suppress and the preliminary hearing."

"Okay Brent. Thank you."

CHAPTER SEVENTEEN

Judge Brian Clark had been on the Santa Barbara Municipal Court bench before all Municipal Courts had become Superior Courts, but the job had not changed much with the change of title. He was still in charge of the court's preliminary hearing mill. He was a balding man in his late 40's, with still some brown hair left, and he had a habit of sucking on cough drops, even when he was on the bench.

In every felony case, a judge had to conduct a preliminary hearing, to determine if there was enough cause to hold the accused to a trial. It was kind of a one-man show, where the D.A. put on his or her most important witnesses, usually police officers, and the outcome almost always ended in the judge holding the defendant to answer. But it gave the defense a little peek into how those witnesses would act at the trial.

Before the hearing, the judge held a conference in his chambers and went over all the cases on his calendar with the D.A. and defense counsel.

"Who's got the Haskins case?" Clark asked, as he clicked a cough drop around his teeth.

"I do, Your Honor," said Bradley Chernow." Chernow was an aspiring young prosecutor who had his sights on a judicial position, or maybe even politics. He was also an ex-classmate of Brent's from law school. He was clever, sharp, but still had that "cop look" from the days he had served in uniform, and the same style of dress. Brent had always liked Chernow in law school. He had friendly, amber eyes and a pleasant disposition, but they had never really become friends. Brent could never shake the feeling that Chernow thought that he had made it on his own, and that he regarded Brent as coming from privilege – the easy way.

"You're on the defense, right Brent?" asked Judge Clark.

"Yes, Your Honor."

"Is there an offer on this case?"

"Your Honor, we're not prepared to make an offer. It's a capital case," replied Chernow.

"Brad, she's an old lady. Plus, we haven't had an execution in California since 2006. Why don't you plead her out to second degree, and we'll send it for a report?"

"I'll discuss it with my client, Your Honor, but I'm not sure this one is ready to be plead out."

"I agree," said Chernow. "And I'd also have to get authority."

"Well then, you discuss it with your client, and you get authority. Then we'll reconvene and see whether to go forward on this."

Brent had the obligation to relay the proposition to Nancy, but he didn't relish doing that. She was nervous enough already. Brent took Nancy out into his courtroom "office" – the hallway.

Nancy, the Judge has asked me to explore a possible settlement with you, and he's asked the District Attorney to do the same."

"Settlement?"

"Yes. The Judge suggests a plea bargain."

"I remember discussing this with you. Brent, I didn't do it – whatever they say – I'll just throw myself on the mercy of the Court."

"Well, I have to communicate this to you, because, if you're convicted of first degree murder with special circumstances, throwing yourself on the mercy of the Court could get you the death penalty. And if you're convicted of first degree murder, the sentence is life in prison."

"My God! What is their offer?"

"It's not an offer yet, but the judge suggests a plea to second degree murder, which carries a sentence of 15 years before you can be considered for parole."

"Brent, in 15 years, I'll be 88 years old. They may as well give me the death penalty. I say we fight."

"No matter what?"

"No matter what."

Brent honestly was relieved by her answer. Defending a murder case was no stroll in the park, but he never took on a case he didn't think he could win, and he felt good about this one.

"Okay then, let's go get 'em!"

* * *

When the Judge called the case, he first took up the matter of Brent's motion to suppress the evidence taken from Nancy's trash can, which was, essentially, the only physical evidence they had in the case. If this evidence was suppressed, there was no case and it would be dismissed.

"Your Honor, you have the motion before you. The defendant in this case had an expectation of privacy in her garbage because it was in her garage and not yet set out for collection. I cited the landmark United States Supreme Court case of *California v. Greenwood* in my brief," said Brent.

"Your Honor, the defendant gave her consent for the search. Therefore, she waived her Fourth Amendment guarantee against unreasonable searches and seizures," Chernow argued.

"Your Honor, the Fourth Amendment protects a person's reasonable expectation of privacy against unreasonable searches and seizures. A warrant is required unless certain exceptions apply, and a police detective who wants to snoop around fishing for evidence without probable cause is not one of those exceptions," said Brent.

"Mrs. Haskins did not consent to the search of her garage or her garbage container, and, as I mentioned earlier, according to prevailing

Supreme Court case law, she had a reasonable expectation of privacy with respect to that garbage can and everything inside of it, unless and until it was placed outside for collection."

"Mr. Chernow?" asked Judge Clark, rolling his cough drop from one cheek to the other.

"Your Honor, the detective asked if he could search the premises, and the defendant consented. She made no objection when he indicated he was going into the garage, so the only reasonable inference we can draw from that is that she consented to a search of the *entire* premises. Consent *is* a recognized exception to the Fourth Amendment guarantee."

"Mr. Marks?"

"Your Honor, under the law, a person's consent has to be the product of his or her own free will and not the mere submission to an assertion of authority. Detective Tomassi had no probable cause whatsoever to believe that evidence of a crime would be found by a search of Mrs. Haskins' home. When he asked if he could 'look around,' Mrs. Haskins asked if she needed a lawyer, and the Detective responded that he didn't think so.

"The scope of the consent to search was never defined, and no consent form was signed. The Detective merely asked if he could 'look around.' Under these circumstances, there cannot be deemed consent to search the garage. 'Looking around' denotes looking around the area of the home where Mrs. Haskins and the Detective were situated, not the garage and certainly not the trash can."

"Mr. Chernow?"

"Your Honor, as you can see from the detective's declaration, he asked if he could look around the defendant's home and the defendant agreed. There was no coercion involved."

"I agree with Mr. Chernow," said the Judge. "The motion to suppress is denied. Are the parties ready for preliminary hearing?"

"Yes, Your Honor."

"Yes, Your Honor."

"The Court will be in recess for 15 minutes and then take up the matter for preliminary hearing."

CHAPTER EIGHTEEN

"The Court calls the case of *People vs. Nancy Haskins*," said the judge, in between clicks and smacks.

"Brent Marks appearing with defendant, who is present in Court, Your Honor."

"Bradley Chernow for the people, Your Honor."

"Thank you Gentlemen. Mr. Chernow, are you ready to proceed?"

"Yes, Your Honor."

"Thank you. Do you have an opening statement?"

"No, Your Honor, I will waive opening statement."

"Please call your first witness."

"Your Honor, I call Dr. Ignacio Perez."

Dr. Perez was sworn in by the clerk, and took a seat in the witness stand. Being a medical examiner for the county, this was routine for him.

"Please state your name for the record."

"My name is Dr. Ignacio Perez."

"Dr. Perez, what is your current occupation?"

"I am a medical examiner for the county of Santa Barbara."

"Can you please summarize for the Court, your education and experience?"

"I am a certified medical examiner, currently serving with the County of Santa Barbara. I hold an M.D. and a PhD from Georgetown University School of Medicine, an A.B. from Dartmouth, and a medical license from the State of California, where I am board certified in clinical, anatomic and forensic pathology. I am a Diplomate of the American Board of Forensic Medicine, and. . ."

"Your Honor, the defense accepts the qualifications of this witness for the purposes of this preliminary hearing, subject to cross examination on his actual findings."

"Very well. Mr. Chernow, you may inquire."

"Dr. Perez, did you perform an autopsy on Barbara Densmore, the victim in this case?"

"Yes, I did."

"And, as a result of that autopsy, did you prepare an autopsy report and a certificate of death?"

"Yes."

"Showing you what has been marked for identification as Exhibits 1 and 2, can you identify Exhibit 1 as a true copy of your report and Exhibit 2 as a true copy of the death certificate?"

"Yes, they are."

"Dr. Perez, were you able to form an opinion, within a degree of reasonable medical certainty of the victim's cause of death?"

"Yes, I was."

"What was the cause of death that you determined?"

"The victim was poisoned."

"Were you able to determine the type of poison?"

"It was ricin poisoning."

"Objection and move to strike!" interjected Brent. "Non-responsive."

"Sustained. It is non-responsive. The answer will be stricken," declared Judge Clark.

"In your opinion, what type of poison was responsible for the victim's death?"

"Objection, lack of foundation," Brent barked out.

"Sustained. Mr. Chernow, for the doctor to have an opinion, it has to be based on evidence, and that evidence must be shown as foundation. You may proceed."

Chernow was getting a little flustered by now. He was no match for Brent in the moot court battles at law school, but had gone on to quite an experienced career as a prosecutor. The old competition had crept back into Brent's skin and he wouldn't back down. Nancy was openly pleased. She smiled at Brent and whispered, "You're doing great!" Brent put his hand on her arm and whispered back, "Thanks, but remember, I told you not to expect much from this."

Chernow continued, "Dr. Perez, as a result of your examination, did you come to the conclusion that Ms. Densmore had been poisoned?"

"Objection, asked and answered!" said Brent, just to get Chernow flustered.

"It has been asked and answered, Mr. Chernow," said the judge.

Chernow's cheeks were flushed. Nancy was so happy she was wiggling in her chair.

"It's foundational, Your Honor."

"Very well, overruled. You may continue."

"Dr. Perez, as a result of your examination, you came to the conclusion that Ms. Densmore had been poisoned, is that correct?"

Brent could not resist. "Leading, Your Honor," he barked out. Chernow glared at him.

"It is leading, but I'll allow it. Mr. Chernow, please try to keep this tighter. I have a large calendar today."

"Yes, Your Honor."

"I concluded from my examination, yes, that Ms. Densmore had been poisoned."

"On what did you base that opinion?"

"On the symptoms I had observed from the autopsy. She had lesions on her esophagus, complete respiratory failure, and she was foaming at the mouth shortly before death."

"Were you able to determine the poison from the examination?"

"No, I was not."

"Did you perform toxicology tests to determine the poison?"

"Yes."

"And what did the tests show?"

"They all came back negative."

"And what did that lead you to conclude, if anything?"

"It led me to conclude that it was a poison that would not show up on a blood test. That, and the symptoms she exhibited were why I suspected it was ricin."

"Move to strike the last sentence, Your Honor, lack of foundation."

"It will be stricken."

Chernow gave Brent another dirty look. *Why take it so personally?* Brent thought. *I'm the one with the client facing the death penalty, not him.* The bottom line was that Brent had uncovered the weakness of this witness; something he had already known from the discovery he had received from the D.A.'s office. Dr. Perez knew that Densmore had been poisoned and he knew it was ricin, but, without further physical evidence, he couldn't prove it.

"Dr. Perez, in cases where you cannot determine the type of poison, is there a forensic protocol, and, if so, what is it?" asked Chernow.

"Yes, the protocol is to examine the death scene to determine the presence of any poisons."

"Thank you, Dr. Perez."

"Anything further of this witness, Mr. Chernow?"

"No, Your Honor."

"Cross examination, Mr. Marks?"

"Yes, thank you, Your Honor. Dr. Perez, isn't it true that you could not determine from the toxicology report that the poison that killed Ms. Densmore was ricin?"

"Yes, that is true."

"And isn't it also true that the only way to confirm your opinion that the poison that caused Ms. Densmore's death is to determine if ricin was found at the death scene?"

"We also sent a urine sample to CDC for testing, but we're still waiting for the results."

"So, without that report, in order to confirm your hunch that Ms. Densmore died from ricin poisoning, you would have to find traces of ricin at the scene of her death, isn't that correct?"

"It's not a hunch," said the Doctor, wrinkling his forehead in frustration.

"Move to strike as non-responsive, Your Honor," said Brent.

"Doctor, please answer the question," said the Judge.

"But I can't answer it yes or no."

"Then please just answer it."

"The answer to your question, Mr. Marks, is that to confirm my diagnosis of ricin poisoning, it is true that we would have to find traces of ricin in the environment."

"Thank you Doctor. Your Honor, I have no further questions of this witness."

"Mr. Chernow?"

"No further questions, Your Honor."

"Well then, Dr. Perez you may be excused. Please call your next witness, Mr. Chernow."

Dr. Perez stepped down from the stand, gave a smile to Brent as he passed by, and Chernow called his next witness.

CHAPTER NINETEEN

"I call Detective Roland Tomassi."

Detective Tomassi approached the witness stand, faced the clerk, took the oath, and sat down.

"Mr. Chernow, you may inquire."

"Thank you, Your Honor. Detective Tomassi, will you please state your full name?"

"My name is Roland Tomassi."

"And you are a California Peace Officer?"

"Yes, I am."

"What is your current assignment?"

"I am a detective in the Homicide Division of the Santa Barbara County Sheriff's Department."

"And how long have you been serving as detective in the Homicide Division?"

"About 20 years, give or take a few months," said Tomassi, dryly.

"And you are also the officer who was first on the scene at Barbara Densmore's house after her death, is that correct?"

"Yes."

Tomassi described the scene, his interview with Nancy, the search of her house and the arrest, in detail, as well as the positive test for ricin on the cellophane wrapping and flower food package.

"Cross examination, Mr. Marks?"

"Thank you, Your Honor. Detective Tomassi, isn't it true that the forensic team you described made a thorough search of Barbara Densmore's residence for evidence?"

"Yes, sir."

"And you specifically instructed them that you were looking for some type of poison, isn't that correct?"

"Yes, sir."

"And isn't it also correct that, all the interviews of witnesses that you have conducted indicated that Barbara Densmore was at home all day before being taken to the hospital in the ambulance?"

"That is correct, sir."

"So there is no doubt in your mind that she would have ingested the poison at her residence, isn't that correct?"

"Objection, calls for speculation," Chernow interjected.

"He can answer if he has an opinion," said the Judge. "Detective Tomassi, answer the question if you can."

"No, sir, there is no doubt in my mind that it occurred at her residence."

"Is it also true that, at her residence, your forensic team found no traces of ricin?"

"Yes, that is true."

"And they also found no traces of any poison of any kind, isn't that correct?"

"Yes, that is correct."

"You testified, Detective Tomassi that, as a result of a search of Mrs. Haskin's house that you did find cellophane wrapping in her garbage can with traces of ricin on it, is that correct?"

"Yes, that is correct."

"And this cellophane wrapping had no fingerprints besides the victim's, isn't that correct?"

"That is correct."

"This means that, if anyone had wiped the cellophane clean, they would have done so only before Barbara Densmore handled it, isn't that correct?"

"Objection, calls for speculation," Chernow called out.

"It does call for speculation, but the inference is there," said the Judge. "And this is just a preliminary hearing. You can answer."

"It seems that, if fingerprints were wiped, they were done before Ms. Densmore handled it, yes."

"And, by the same token, they could not have been wiped clean *after* because that would have also wiped Ms. Densmore's prints off, isn't that correct?"

"It seems so, yes. But the suspect could have used gloves to handle the cellophane to avoid leaving prints."

"One more question, Detective Tomassi. Did you find any flowers at Ms. Haskin's residence?"

"No."

After the short cross examination, Chernow tried to introduce Barbara Densmore's sister to identify a picture of her body, but Brent stipulated and agreed that it was, indeed, a photograph of Barbara Densmore. He didn't see the need of putting the sister through that.

CHAPTER TWENTY

Jack set upon the boring task of following the leads on the neighbors, no matter how cold he thought they were. He had done a background check on each one of them. Gary Goldstein had a minor criminal record back in New York. Seems he had an anger management problem and not only had slapped his wife around a couple of times, he had gotten into it with one of his neighbors in the Queens neighborhood they lived in.

Jack had set up surveillance on Goldstein. It was pretty uneventful during the daytime. He went to his nine to five office job in a Santa Barbara accountancy firm, and had lunch every day with a female co-worker. Maybe he was having an affair with her.

He had a few hours today before Goldstein would come home, so he decided to interview Jean Goldstein. Jean was a housewife. One kid was deceased, the other grown, and since then, she never had transitioned from being a mother/housewife to anything else.

"I told everything to the police, Detective Ruder," she said to Jack.

"I'm a private detective, ma'am. I work for Brent Marks, the defense counsel for Nancy Haskins."

"Oh, I heard about that. Isn't it awful? To think that there's a murderer living in our own development?"

"Exactly, ma'am. We're just trying to uncover the truth."

"Well isn't it pretty clear? I read that she was charged with murder and the judge found her guilty."

"No ma'am, that was just a preliminary hearing. There's going to be a murder trial."

Jean offered Jack a cup of coffee, something that he found impossible to refuse, since he had been living on it night and day during his stakeouts. He learned the story of the death of their son as well as the battle with the Homeowners Association over his memorial. He learned that Jean's husband, Gary had had a few scrapes with Densmore, and that he had actually threatened her a couple of times. Suddenly, everything started to make sense to Jack. He gingerly pressed her for what she may know about the Densmore case.

Jean didn't seem to know much of anything about the Densmore murder. Either she was completely innocent, or a pathological liar. In Jack's business, you could never be sure. Human nature being what it was, the only time you could really be sure you weren't being lied to was when you were talking to yourself.

As Jack pulled out to head back to Goldstein's office to pick up the surveillance trail, he noticed Gary Goldstein pulling up. At least he knew where Goldstein would be for at least the next few hours. To avoid being made, he circled around the block, and parked about half a block away and stopped. He sat in his car and killed the time going over the surveillance files he had compiled on all the neighbors. He was already stoked up by the coffee that Jean had served him during their talk. It would be a long night.

* * *

It didn't take long for Goldstein to be on the move again. He had developed some late night habits, apparently waiting for his wife to go to sleep so he could pursue his affair. All this late night surveillance had also developed some poor late night habits in Jack as well.

Jack followed Goldstein to an apartment complex in Santa Barbara and was munching on a Wendy's chicken burger when he noticed Goldstein leaving. Jack set the burger down on the passenger seat and took off after Goldstein. Halfway down Garden Street, Goldstein stopped in the middle of the street.

Shit, he made me! Thought Jack to himself. Sure enough, Goldstein slammed his Ford F-250 into reverse, wheels burning against the asphalt, and screeched to a halt inches away from Jack's bumper. Leaving the car running, he ran to Jack's car and pounded against the driver's side window. His wild, chestnut eyes looked empty and his mouth was open so wide, Jack could have sworn Goldstein's intention was to take a bite out of him, or his car.

"Come on! Come on!" he screamed, saliva spraying from the side of his mouth. Jack jammed his car in reverse and Goldstein ran after it for a couple of seconds, then got back in his car and took chase. After weaving through a couple of streets, Jack either lost the tail or Goldstein gave up.

When Jack got home, he called Brent right away and left a message on his voice mail.

"Hey Brent, it's Jack. I know you're probably asleep already but I think I've developed a good lead on Gary Goldstein. Maybe we can get together tomorrow night? Give me a call."

CHAPTER TWENTY-ONE

Brent had sequestered himself in his office to make the last minute preparations. He had organized the entire trial into notebook binders – binders containing all the exhibits, binders with the briefs and jury instructions, and binders with Brent's direct and cross examination outlines, opening statements and closing arguments. A criminal trial had a higher standard of proof than a civil trial. The state had to prove every element of its case beyond a reasonable doubt, or Nancy would be acquitted. And the verdict of the jury had to be unanimous. All twelve jurors had to vote for a conviction, or Nancy would be acquitted. The jury system was somewhat of an anomaly, like everything else in the law. A defendant put his or her fate in the hands of twelve strangers, who had no legal training, but who were expected to carefully listen to the evidence from two points of view, get a one hour education on what highly complex principles of law to apply to the evidence, and then make a unanimous decision. The lawyers always had a chance to talk to the jury members after a trial was over. After doing it many times, Brent usually opted out because most of the time, nothing they said made any sense. It was ridiculous for Brent to think that twelve people could "turn off" all their biases and prejudices and make a logical decision based on the evidence they were allowed to hear in the trial. But, however strange it seemed, Brent knew that sometimes you had a better shot with a jury, that body of ones "peers" who make decisions with their emotional brains; especially if your client was guilty.

Nancy was not obligated to say anything; she had the Fifth Amendment privilege against self-incrimination. But Brent knew that the jury would need to hear her side of the story, even though the judge would instruct them that the burden was entirely on the prosecution to prove 100% of its case. It was human nature. He took extra time to prepare Nancy. It almost didn't matter what she said. She could say anything at all; the jury just had to get a feel for her as a real person; they had to *care* about her.

Trials for lawyers are like bills. It seems that you finish paying one, and have that feeling of relief, then it's time to pay it again. It had been a while since Brent's last criminal trial, but he was confident. It was like swimming – you never really forget how to do it no matter how long it's been. No clear cut alternative suspects could be presented to the jury, nor he did have any evidence of a frame to present, the D.A.'s case was all based on circumstantial evidence. Brent's job was to poke as many holes in their case that he could.

* * *

Brent left the office on foot for his meeting with Jack at Sonny's on downtown State Street. It wasn't too long a distance and a walk was better than anything to clear the mind for new thoughts.

Sonny's was always packed. Being at the end of State Street, the cops had parked several squad cars in the neighborhood, perhaps as a deterrent for drunk drivers, or to give them something to do around closing time.

As Brent rolled into Sonny's, he felt a nostalgic, melancholic feeling. This was the favorite bar of his good friend, Rick Penn, who had been gone for a couple of years now. Rick was also a private detective and ex-FBI man, and they had spent many a night here going over cases, among other things. So, as sad as it may have been, perhaps it was also a good place to work. A lot of ideas had been thrown back and forth between Brent and Rick through the years, and it happened right there at Sonny's.

Brent found Jack at the bar, looking pretty worn out. Jack smiled as Brent approached and took a seat next to him.

"Hey Brent," Jack greeted him.

"What's up Jack, have you solved my case yet?"

"Unfortunately, no. I've been running surveillance on Gary Goldstein. I told you he had a minor criminal record in New York."

Brent waved to the bartender and ordered a margarita, and Jack recounted the incident with Goldstein.

"So, anything promising on Mr. Road Rage?" asked Brent.

"Not yet. We've got some pretty vivid descriptions of him threatening Densmore, but that's about it so far."

"Yeah, well he is from New York."

"Right. His idea of saying hello is 'fuck you.'"

The comment made Brent burst out in laughter, and the funniest part was that Jack said it so straight-faced. Brent couldn't stop laughing and Jack caught the laugh and belly laughed until tears came to his eyes.

"Damn Jack," said Brent, taking a generous sip from his Margarita, "I honestly didn't think you had it in you. What's that you're drinking, coffee?"

"Yeah, I'm going back to pick up Goldstein's trail. Can't drink and drive."

"Well, I'm taking a cab home, but I'm going to take it easy too. Trial starts tomorrow."

"I'll get something. I never give up."

"I know, Jack."

Brent paid the bar tab, they both got up from the bar, and Brent slapped Jack on the back.

"Want a ride, Brent? My car's out back in the parking lot."

"No buddy, I think I'll walk back to the office before I go home. Walking's a great way to create. The ideas seem to fall from the sky sometimes, and the fresh air is great too."

"Suit yourself."

Jack walked out the back door into the parking lot. As Brent started to leave through the front, it didn't take long for a thought to pop into his head, so he ran out back to see if he could catch Jack to ask him a question.

When Brent ran out the back door, he almost bumped into Jack, who seemed to be in a Mexican standoff with a disheveled and very drunk looking Gary Goldstein. The moonlight danced and gleamed off the shiny blade of a large knife Goldstein was holding in his hand.

"Who hired you?" Goldstein screamed, spittle flying. "My wife?"

"I did Goldstein," said Brent. "Now drop the knife and back off, unless you want to get arrested for felony assault and spend the next five years in prison."

"And what if I don't?" he had the nerve to ask.

"Then I'll have to take that knife away from you and stick it in your neck," said Jack, calmly and matter-of-factly, as if it were something he was used to doing.

Goldstein looked at Jack, then at Brent, dropped the knife and ran away.

"Call 911," said Jack, who ran after him.

CHAPTER TWENTY-TWO

The Santa Barbara Courthouse was a brilliant piece of California Spanish Colonial architecture that had been in place since the days of Clarence Darrow. It was a lovely building with arched corridors and an exquisite courtyard garden. It was so beautiful, that one being forced to jury duty there may actually enjoy it. Brent loved having a trial there because he felt as if he could feel a whole century's worth of great minds who had tried cases there, like Melvin Belli and F. Lee Bailey. These adobe plastered and wood paneled walls had heard scores of brilliant and eloquent orations throughout the years.

The old wooden benches in the spectator gallery gave the courtroom more of a church feel than a courtroom. Brent and Nancy settled into their chairs at the counsel table just after the doors of the courtroom opened. Brent got out his master trial notebook and turned to the outline for *voir dire*, a set of questions he had prepared to ask potential jury members. Judge Hanford Curtis, the judge assigned to the trial, had already heard all the preliminary *motions in limine*. He was a firm but soft-spoken African American jurist, who had been on the bench for over 20 years. There would be no business today except for choosing a jury. Bradley Chernow came in and took his seat. There were only a few observers in the galley.

"Morning Brad," said Brent.

"Brent."

"All rise!" said the Clerk. Everyone stood.

"The Superior Court for the State of California for the County of Santa Barbara is now in session, the Honorable Hanford Curtis, Judge presiding."

"Good morning ladies and gentlemen," said the Judge. "Please be seated. We are on the record today in the case of *People v. Haskins*. Counsel, please state your appearances."

"Brent Marks for the Defendant, Nancy Haskins, who is present in court, Your Honor."

"Good morning, Your Honor. Bradley Chernow for the people."

"Thank you, Mr. Marks and Mr. Chernow. We've had a conference and a pretrial hearing and I think we've gotten all the preliminaries out of the way. Am I correct?"

All counsel answered yes.

"Alright, it appears there are no further matters for the Court to consider before proceeding to jury selection. Madame Clerk, will you please send in the first panel?"

The gallery filled up with about three dozen prospective jurors, and the Clerk called the first twelve, who had been chosen by random. They filled up the twelve of the fourteen chairs in the jury box; the two extra being for the selection of alternate jurors, in case a juror was sick or could not serve for some other reason. All jurors had filled out questionnaires which were given to Brent and to the D.A. Brent immediately turned a copy of the questionnaire over to Jack, who ran out to perform quick background checks on the entire panel. The Judge read a statement of the case which had been prepared and agreed upon by both counsel during the pretrial conference, and asked the jurors to answer some basic questions that were on display on a chart in front of the jury box, such as age, occupation, and family background. Both counsel would be looking for biases and prejudices. In this game, the Judge wanted each juror to be fair and unbiased, and each attorney wanted a juror that would not be biased against their case, but perhaps have a tinge of bias in favor of it.

* * *

Brent was looking for jurors who had had bad experiences with homeowners associations. He knew that was too ideal, because Chernow would use all of his peremptory challenges to kick off any prospective juror whoever had a problem with an HOA. But Brent would also be looking for jurors who knew someone who had been involved with an HOA. There wasn't a chance for many because Santa Barbara didn't have many new real estate developments. Most housing was at least 30 years old, and that was young for Santa Barbara. Brent was also looking for older people, perhaps widows or widowers, who would have sympathy for Nancy due to her age and position in life. Luckily for Brent, most of the people who were sitting in the box would either be retired, unemployed or their employment encouraged jury duty and they were on a kind of "paid vacation" in court.

After the jurors finished answering the Judge's questions, the Judge turned it over to the attorneys for the *voir dire* inquiry into the prospective juror's backgrounds. Because it was a capital case, each side was given a total of 20 peremptory challenges to potential jurors, which allowed the lawyer to kick any juror off the panel without giving a reason. Each lawyer could make a motion to dismiss a juror for cause as well, but it was rarely, if ever, done.

"Mr. Chernow, the people have the floor," said the Judge.

"Thank you, Your Honor. Ladies and gentlemen, if you're chosen to serve on this jury, the Judge will instruct you that circumstantial evidence is evidence that does not directly prove a fact to be decided, but is evidence of another fact or group of facts from which you may logically and reasonably conclude the truth of the fact in question. He will also instruct you that facts can be proved by circumstantial evidence, direct evidence or a combination of both. Do any of you feel that you could not make a logical and reasonable conclusion from only circumstantial evidence? If so, please raise your hands."

Of course, nobody raised their hand. Chernow was not playing dirty, but he was planting seeds in the juror's minds because he knew that a tremendously big jump had to be made to infer that Nancy was the murderer because the only real evidence against her was the clear plastic wrapping from the flowers that had been found in her garbage can.

Chernow went through an exhaustive list of questions with the potential jurors, and it seemed he would never stop. Finally, he came to the most important question.

"Juror number 12, Antonio Jalisco. Mr. Jalisco, as the Court informed you, this is a capital case, where the penalty for guilt may be death. If you thought that someone was guilty of premeditated murder and that it had been proven without a reasonable doubt, would you have any problem voting guilty knowing that the person could be sentenced to death?"

"No, I would not," replied Mr. Jalisco.

Chernow varied his questions for each juror, but he posed this particular one to every juror. One of them, juror number 6, Helen Wyndam, had very strong religious convictions and could not vote guilty if it meant the defendant could possibly be put to death.

CHAPTER TWENTY-THREE

Jack noticed that the VW van was parked in the driveway at Keith Michel's, so he knocked on the door. Michel answered the door, dressed in a white tee shirt and shorts, with messy hair and sleepy eyes. It looked like he had either just woken up or had just gone to bed. *Typical druggie,* thought Jack.

"Mr. Michel?"

"Who wants to know?"

Jack put out his card. "Jack Ruder, private investigator."

"What's this about?" Michel asked, wiggling like he had to go to the bathroom.

"I was attacked by one of your roommates the other night."

"Way I heard it, dude, you were trespassing."

"Who else lives here with you, Mr. Michel?"

"Well there's Manny."

Jack took down the name in his notebook.

"What's his last name?"

"Dude, I don't know. I'm not a census taker. All I care about is the rent. Cash is king."

"So your roommates are your tenants?"

"Yeah."

"Who else lives here with you?"

"Well, there's Moe."

Jack started to write down the name, "Moe," and then stopped and looked up at Michel, who was wearing a shit-eating grin.

"Let me guess, you don't know Moe's last name either, right?"

"Dude, you're good!"

"And your other roommate's name must be Jack, right? Manny, Moe and Jack?"

"Dude, it's like you're a psychic or something."

"Thanks for your cooperation, Mr. Michel," Jack said, and turned to leave.

"Anytime, dude!"

* * *

After the lunch break, Brent was given the floor, and tried to fuse the principle of reasonable doubt with the principle of circumstantial evidence in the minds of the jurors. His job during the trial would be to drive a wedge of reasonable doubt into every piece of circumstantial evidence that he could.

"Ladies and gentlemen of the panel, when my colleague Mr. Chernow spoke to you about circumstantial evidence, he explained how the Court would instruct you what it was and how it can be used to draw an inference about a proven fact. However, the Judge will also instruct you that before you may rely on circumstantial evidence to conclude that a fact necessary to find the defendant guilty has been proved, you must be convinced that the People have proved each fact essential to that conclusion beyond a reasonable doubt. Who knows what that means?"

A man in the panel raised his hand.

"Juror number four, Mr. Samuels, what do you think reasonable doubt means?"

"It means you have to be sure about it."

"The Judge will tell you what the law says reasonable doubt is. He will instruct you that the defendant is presumed innocent and that the People have the burden of proving beyond a reasonable doubt that it was the defendant who committed the crime. They must prove this as to every element of the crime, and if they don't, you have to acquit my client. He will instruct you that the defendant does not have to say anything or prove anything. The entire burden is on the People. With that in mind, does anybody on the panel think they would have to hear the defendant's side of the story to decide anything?"

Two hands shot up and Brent took notes of who they were.

"The Judge will tell you that the reasonable doubt standard is more stringent than the preponderance of evidence standard we use in a civil case. The preponderance of evidence standard asks you to decide whether the evidence shows that a fact is more likely than not true. The reasonable doubt standard goes one step further. It asks you to decide whether each essential element of the case has been proved by the People to the point of an abiding conviction in you that the charge is true. Does anybody not understand this concept?"

Juror number 7, Joseph Baker, raised his hand.

Brent continued to question the jurors until he had run out of questions, then informed the Judge.

"The Court will hear any challenges for cause," said Judge Curtis.

"Pass for cause, Your Honor," said Brent.

"Pass for cause, Your Honor," said Chernow.

"Alright then, the first peremptory challenge is with the People."

"The People wish to thank and excuse Juror No. 6, Mrs. Helen Wyndam."

Ms. Wyndam was excused, and the clerk drew another potential juror's name from the gallery, filling her empty seat. This began a process of questioning the next prospective juror, who took a seat in the jury box and underwent the entire *voir dire* process.

"The next peremptory challenge is with the Defendant."

"The Defendant wishes to thank and excuse Juror No. 7, Joseph Baker."

Jury selection continued through the end of the day and into the next, until all 40 peremptory challenges had been used. The final jury was composed of five men, seven women and two alternates; one man and one woman. To Brent's delight, most of the members of the jury had grey hair.

"Madame Clerk, please swear in the jury," instructed Judge Curtis. The swearing was followed by the traditional admonishments, prohibiting the jurors from talking to anyone about the case, even amongst themselves. Then Judge Curtis turned to the lawyers and asked, "Mr. Marks, Mr. Chernow, is there anything else to bring before the Court's attention before we start?"

"Yes, Your Honor, I move that witnesses be excluded from the Courtroom except during their testimony," said Chernow.

"Any objection, Mr. Marks?"

"No, Your Honor."

"Motion granted."

Then Court was adjourned to the following day for the real work to begin.

* * *

If home is a state of mind, Brent slipped into it even before he pulled up to his Harbor Hills Drive home. After he got in and fed the cat, he relaxed and had a drink on the patio and looked at the ocean for a while. It was a calming end to a hectic day, and there were even more hectic days to come.

Brent spent some time after dinner going over his outlines for the opening statement and cross examination of witnesses. You never could be ready enough for a trial, but he was going to be as ready as he possibly could.

CHAPTER TWENTY-FOUR

Bradley Chernow stood in front of the jury at the podium confidently. He had done this many times, and had his cookie-cutter analogies all set to go. With his opening statement, the first battle of the war had begun.

"Ladies and gentlemen of the jury. This is the guilt phase of the trial, where you will be asked to decide whether the defendant, Nancy Haskins, murdered the victim, Barbara Densmore, by poison, which is a special circumstance under the law which could lead the defendant to a sentence of life in prison or the death penalty. As the Judge will instruct you, you are not to consider the possible penalty in making your decision on whether the defendant is guilty or not guilty of this heinous crime.

"As the Judge also will instruct you, the People have the burden of proving their case beyond a reasonable doubt. That doesn't mean that you must have no doubts at all about the evidence; it simply means that from the evidence you consider, you must decide whether, to an abiding conviction, that the charge is true."

As he spoke, Chernow made eye contact with each person in the jury, to make them comfortable and at ease with him, but also so he could see whether he was getting through to them. So far, it looked as if they were following him alright.

"We talked a lot about circumstantial evidence during the jury section. Most cases only have circumstantial evidence. It's very rare when you have an actual eyewitness to a crime who can tell you everything that happened.

"A case is kind of like a puzzle. When you start with the puzzle and pour the puzzle pieces out of the box, it's just a bunch of colored pieces all jumbled up, and doesn't resemble a picture at all. But, as you complete the puzzle, you can begin to see what the picture is. Once you've reached that point, you can tell, more likely than not, what the picture is. At that point, you are at what the law calls the "preponderance of the evidence" standard. Once the puzzle becomes clear and you have an abiding conviction as to what the picture actually is, you have reached the reasonable doubt standard. There may be pieces of the puzzle that are missing here and there, but you know for sure what the picture is.

"The People will present evidence that on May 3rd of this year, Nancy Haskins, with the intent to kill Barbara Densmore, delivered a bouquet of flowers to her that were specially rigged to dispense a fatal poison called ricin, and that this, in fact, killed Barbara Densmore. You will hear testimony from Barbara's colleague, Frances Templeton, who will tell you about death threats which Mrs. Haskins made to her.

"You will hear the testimony of Detective Roland Tomassi of the Santa Barbara Sheriff's Dept. that cellophane wrapping used to wrap the deadly flowers was found in Ms. Haskin's garbage, which had traces of the poison ricin. You will hear testimony from Dr. Ignacio Perez, the medical examiner, who will testify that this poison caused the death of Ms. Densmore."

Chernow then directed his gaze to Nancy at the counsel table, as if he was hurling the accusation straight at her body.

"The People are confident that, after hearing all of this testimony and examining all of the evidence, you will be convinced beyond a reasonable doubt that Nancy Haskins committed the crime of the murder of Barbara Densmore by poison. Thank you."

"Mr. Marks, do you wish to give an opening statement or reserve it to your case-in-chief?" asked Judge Curtis.

"I'd like to give an opening statement now, Your Honor," Brent replied.

"Very well, please proceed."

Brent walked up to the podium, rested his arm on it, and spoke to the jury as if he were talking to a group of friends.

"Ladies and gentlemen, I represent Nancy Haskins, the defendant. As you've all been briefed during the jury selection, for the first part of this case, we're going to listen to all the evidence that the D.A. has gathered concerning this case to determine whether the D.A. has proven every element of murder beyond a reasonable doubt.

"Now this is not a very easy thing to do, because all of the evidence you are going to hear is going to be circumstantial evidence. The prosecution claims that Barbara Densmore was presented with a bouquet of flowers, and that bouquet of flowers contained a deadly poison called ricin, but there is no evidence of any flowers, and no evidence of any delivery of flowers. The only evidence that exists is cellophane wrapping and a package of flower food containing ricin with only Ms. Densmore's fingerprints on it.

"The Judge will tell you that the People must prove every element of their case beyond a reasonable doubt. That means that they have to present evidence from which you can infer without a reasonable doubt that: 1) Nancy Haskins had the intent to kill Barbara Densmore; 2) that she did, in fact, kill her, by administering a deadly poison; and 3) that this resulted in her death.

"All of this has to be proven by the prosecution, and the defense does not have an obligation to prove *anything*. But, ladies and gentlemen, the defense will go farther than that. Even though Mrs. Haskins has no obligation to, and, in fact the *right* not to testify in her defense, she is going to testify and tell you that she had *nothing* to do with this horrible murder.

"The Judge will instruct you, ladies and gentlemen, that, if there are two inferences you can draw from the evidence you hear and see; one of which leads to the conclusion that Mrs. Haskins is guilty, and one of which leads to the conclusion that she is *not* guilty, that you must select the inference that leads to the conclusion that she is not guilty. I am confident that, after hearing and seeing all of the evidence, that you will have no choice but to choose the inference that Mrs. Haskins is not guilty. Her life is in your hands. Thank you."

"Objection! Move to strike as prejudicial!" called out Chernow.

"Counsel approach the bench," said the Judge.

"Good job Brent!" Nancy whispered to Brent as he stood up. Brent suppressed his smile and walked up to the bench, where Chernow was already waiting, eager for the Judge to lambaste him.

"Well, we're not starting out very well, are we?" said Judge Curtis. "Mr. Marks, you know that the jury is not to consider punishment in this phase of the trial."

"Sorry, Your Honor."

"Sorry's not good enough. When something's broken, sorry can never bring it back. Now I know your case is important, and that you're zealous in your defense of your client, but I don't want to declare a mistrial in this case. So please, don't make any more inappropriate comments."

"Yes, Your Honor."

The lawyers went back to their seats and the Judge faced the jury and said, "The motion to strike is granted. The jury is instructed to disregard Mr. Marks' comment that you hold the defendant's life in your hands. It is improper as you are not allowed to consider punishment in reaching a guilty or not guilty verdict in this case."

Nancy leaned over to Brent and whispered, "How can they disregard what they've already heard?"

"They can't," said Brent. "And now they've heard it twice." He winked.

"Ladies and gentlemen, you are excused. I will remind you of your obligation not to talk to counsel or the parties, not to discuss this case amongst yourselves, nor with anyone. Court is adjourned," said Judge Curtis, who stood up, and walked into his chambers, shaking his head.

CHAPTER TWENTY-FIVE

Jack Ruder had spent weeks exhausting all the leads he had for Brent, each one of them cold, and Brent had already started the trial. He had been following the comings and goings at Keith Michel's house for the past 10 days with no luck, and this night was no exception. Stakeouts were incredibly boring. The coffee was bad, the junk food was worse, and his Kindle battery had just died. *Oh well, I guess it's time to call it a night,* he thought, when he noticed the classic tan VW van exit the garage. It was loaded up with surfboards. Jack slumped down in his seat and noted there were four occupants in the vehicle. He waited until the van turned the corner, then pulled out after it.

Once out of the development, the van turned left on Hollister, and Jack stayed far enough behind so he could not be seen, but not far enough to lose them at one of the long traffic signals on Hollister. The van took a right onto Cathedral Oaks and an almost immediate left onto Calle Real. Just as Jack thought he may lose it, it merged onto the northbound 101 freeway.

On the freeway, the van was easier to follow. Jack made sure to keep behind it in the middle lane, about five car lengths back. That way, he would have time to follow the van when it exited the freeway. A few more car lengths behind and exiting would be impossible. So far, the van was staying in the far left lane, so Jack had no trouble keeping an eye on it.

After passing El Capitan Beach, the van exited on Gaviota Beach Road. This confirmed to Jack that they were on a late night surfing trip and that Jack was most likely wasting his time. They passed Gaviota Beach, turning right on Hollister Ranch Road, which had no traffic at all to hide behind, so Jack stayed far behind. After a couple of miles, the van turned onto a desolate dirt road and crossed the railroad tracks. Jack quickly looked for a vantage point, and found one that was high enough, where he could park and use his night vision binoculars to watch the goings on.

When Jack saw the four exit the van and Michel and another dishwater blond surfer type take their surfboards from the roof rack, he figured the game was over, but decided to wait it out. He wasn't really sleepy yet and it had been a long drive, preceded by an even longer wait. He watched the two take off down the beach, jump into the water and start paddling, while their friend, the fat Hispanic guy who had attacked him and another guy sat around smoking. *Not much fun for them,* he thought, as he wondered why all four were not surfing. Jack lost sight of the paddlers a couple of times, but kept scanning the horizon until he could spot them from time to time. He knew that this was a popular surf area with the surf addicts, but because of its inaccessibility, most surfers rode the reefs to the north of Refugio.

Jack sat there, eating the last sticky, stale donut from the box, and intermittently looking at the two pot smokers by the van and the others in the ocean, when he noticed a boat on the horizon. He couldn't quite make it out because it was so far away, but the surfers seemed to be paddling to it. Then another boat appeared, as if out of nowhere. Jack put down the binoculars and got out his long range, night vision video camera. He started to tape the goings on. Michel boarded the first boat, along with his surfboard; then the other surfer boarded the second one.

As the boats drew closer, Jack zoomed in on them to see what was going on. The boats seemed to be about 30-40 feet long in Jack's estimate. He could make out the "Chris-Craft" insignia on each of them. He tried to zoom in on the names of the boats, but he could not see them from his point of view. They were both flying American flags and both towing very large tender boats. Not much was happening with the boats as they drew closer to the shore.

When they were about 100 yards from shore, the boats each dropped their anchor and, at about the same time, Jack saw another VW van, this one blue, pull up alongside the surfer van and park. Four more people hopped out of it; they looked like they were Hispanic. Jack got a close shot of each one of the suspects, and focused in on the van, noting its California license plate, DGY 145. Jack divided his video time between what was going on around the vans and what was happening on the boats.

After the boats were anchored, the crews on both boats began to load the tender boats with bags. Jack could not see the content of the bags, but he could see that it took at least one man to lift one bag. They looked like sacks of potatoes. Several men on each boat formed a conveyor line to load the bags from the boats onto the tender boats. Jack could recognize one of his surfers on each boat, because they were the ones wearing wetsuits.

When the tender boats were loaded, they motored to shore with the two surfers. On the shoreline, what Jack thought before were pot smokers turned out to be a fine-tuned labor force which unloaded the boats with dispatch into the vans. The tender boats returned to the yachts and came back with another load for the vans. Once they had emptied the entire loads of the boats, the surfers returned to the yachts in the tender boats and paddled back on their surfboards. All in all, it had taken the boats about 30 minutes to anchor and transfer their loads to the two vans.

Once the surfers reached the shore, they ran to the van, strapped their surfboards to the rack, jumped in, and both vans were on the move again. Jack couldn't call for "backup," because there was no backup. He wasn't an agent of the FBI anymore, so his only option was to call the police like any ordinary citizen who had witnessed a crime. He figured that, by the time he was able to explain what he had seen to the police, he would lose the vans, so he stuck to the surveillance task he had set out to complete. He would shoot each one of the suspects as best as he could, follow them and try to get them unloading their cargo, then turn copies of everything over to the police.

The vans both took off in synchronized fashion, back to the freeway. One van went northbound, and the surfer van southbound, so Jack decided to stick with the surfers. The van exited the freeway at Hollister and pulled into an EZ Storage facility. Jack pulled his car into an adjacent gas station where he could not be seen, and continued to film the suspects. He got a good shot of each of them as they unloaded the bags into storage unit 331-C.

Wait a minute, thought Jack. *There's only three of them. I wonder where…*

Suddenly Jack looked up from his camera and was face to face with the gun-wielding Hispanic guy from the house, whom Jack already knew had no sense of humor. He waved the gun at Jack.

"Gimme the camera, cabron," the man demanded.

CHAPTER TWENTY-SIX

There was no time to think, only to react. Jack thrust the camera at the man though the car window, and the man instinctively grabbed it. Jack threw open the door, knocking him and the camera down. He looked like a huge turtle that had been knocked on its shell. In that same split second, Jack jumped on him like a wild animal, disarmed him, kicked his gun away and quickly withdrew his stun gun, stuck it against the big man's neck and hit him with over 3 million volts.

The big man's head dropped like a cow being stunned in a slaughterhouse. As his body was still convulsing, Jack took some twist-ties from his utility pack and bound his hands. He whipped off his shirt and gagged the man with it. Jack patted down the man's body for weapons and emptied his pockets; wallet, cell phone, keys, loose change. He pocketed the cell phone.

As the man was coming to, Jack ushered him into the back seat of his car at gunpoint, and bound his own ankles with twist ties. He picked up and reactivated his camera, which, miraculously, was still working, so he could see that the suspects were still busy, and used his cell phone to call 911.

"911, what is your emergency?"

"My name is Jack Ruder. I'm a private investigator and ex-FBI agent. I've just been attacked at gunpoint, have subdued my attacker and have him incapacitated. There are three others – all armed. Please send help immediately!"

That was a mouthful for the emergency operator to take at once, so she clarified the details with Jack and assured him that there was help on the way. Jack next called Brent.

"Hey Buddy."

"Hey Jack, how's it goin'?"

"I just got you a boatload of reasonable doubt, but I'm kind of busy right now, could I please speak to Angie?"

"Sure, she's right here."

Brent handed the phone to Angela, who immediately went into crisis mode, noting down the information.

"I'll call everyone, Jack, we will be there," she said and hung up the phone.

Jack turned now to his attacker.

"Nod your head for yes and shake for no. Do you understand?"

The man nodded.

"Do they know I'm here?" The man shook his head.

"Were you sent out to be lookout?" He nodded.

"Do you have anything to communicate with besides your phone?" He shook his head.

"Okay. There are police and FBI on the way. I'm going to ungag you and I want you to call them and ask them how much longer. When they ask you if everything is okay, you say yes, do you understand?" He nodded.

Jack removed the gag and put the cell phone on speaker. He put his gun to the man's temple.

"Incentive to tell them exactly what I told you. What's the number?"

"555-2396."

Jack held the phone to the man's mouth.

* * *

"What's going on?" Brent asked Angela, as she strapped on her flak jacket, gun and holster and pulled her jacket on over it.

"Jack's got a situation and I've called in a team to help him."

"You're going too?"

"I have to help him."

"Then, I'm going with you."

"No way, you stay here. I'll be in numbers, don't worry."

"That's what you said the last time, and you agreed to take a desk job after that."

"Desk or not, Brent, this *is* my job."

With that, Angela was out the door.

* * *

Angela fired up her government issued Crown Victoria and sped off.

"Agent Wollard, requesting status on possible 10-31 at Goleta EZ Storage," she called into the government frequency radio.

"Roger, Agent Wollard, Santa Barbara Sheriff's Department reports officers and SWAT are 10-76, responding."

"Thank you dispatch, what is their 10-77?"

"About fifteen minutes. Agent Wollard, you are advised to wait for SWAT. Do not engage suspects unless you are in danger."

"10-4."

The stranger's phone rang in Jack's pocket.

"Tell them everything is fine," Jack instructed.

Jack knew that his time was running out. He would stick it out as long as possible, but, if he was facing down three guns, the best thing to do would be to abort and leave as soon as possible. He put the man's phone to his cheek.

"Yo, man, what the fuck! Where are you?" crackled the voice over the speakerphone.

"Outside, Homes, jus' like you told me," said the man.

"Well get your ass back here, Bro. We gotta go!"

"Okay, gimme a couple of minutes."

Jack muted the phone. "Tell them you're taking a dump and you'll be there in five minutes."

"What?" said the voice.

"Man, look, I'm takin' a shit. I'll be there as soon as I'm done."

"Man, that's gross! Couldn't you wait? Well, get your nasty ass back here. Is everything okay out there?"

"Yeah, yeah Bro, fine. Everything's cool."

Jack's forehead broke into a sweat as he watched the crew packing the rest of the bags into the shed and close it up.

Where was Angela and the cavalry? Jack looked around and made his escape plan. He had only minutes to spare.

* * *

Angela exited the freeway on Storke Road and took a right on Hollister. She had no way of communicating with Jack, so she had no idea what was going on. As she sped down Hollister, she noticed two black and white units with lights blazing, fall into place behind her.

"Dispatch, this is Agent Wollard, I've got two black and whites in formation. 10-77 – five minutes."

"10-4 Agent Wollard. SWAT is reporting ten minutes. Hold for SWAT."

"Roger that."

* * *

Another Hispanic man came walking out of the EZ Storage lot, this one with a shotgun. He looked to the right and left of the main entrance, and called out.

"Yo, Felipe, where you at Bro?" he said. Then, he noticed Jack and started running toward Jack's car. Jack jammed the car into reverse and backed out onto the street. The windshield exploded and rained pebbles of glass that bounced against the dashboard as Jack ducked and spun the car around. Jack hit the gas and the rear wheels spewed a rubbery cloud of smoke as Jack heard the shotgun go off again and the momentum of the car taking off bounced his passenger around in the back seat.

"You're dead, man!" said Jack's occupant, as the van took chase.

* * *

When Angela pulled up to EZ Storage with two Sheriff's Dept. patrol cars in tow, everything was quiet like nothing had ever happened there. Just piles of scattered rounded shards of safety glass was all she could find.

Jack rang Angela on her cell phone.

"Angie, you were a little late coming to the party. I've got a situation now."

"Talk to me, Jack."

"I'm being pursued by a beige VW van, California personalized license plates, "Sierra-Uniform-Romeo-Foxtrot-Zulu-Uniform-Papa." They are armed and have already taken one shot at me."

"I'll have the Sheriff's Dept. put out an APB. What's your 20?"

"Southbound Hollister approaching Coromar Drive. Wait Angie!"

Jack glanced in the rear view and saw the van turn off.

"They just turned off."

"Do you still have the suspect in custody?"

"Yes."

"We'll find the van. Come on back to the scene and let's get him turned over to the Sheriff."

The SWAT team pulled up in their armored vehicle and a dozen heavily armed men in military fatigues and helmets descended. After being briefed by Angela, they stormed the storage unit. It was as empty as Al Capone's vault.

CHAPTER TWENTY-SEVEN

The big man sat like a caged animal in the interrogation room as Brent, Angela, Jack, and Agent Samuel Nesta from the DEA looked on through a two-way mirror. He was fidgeting and wiggling his lardy body in the chair, and rubbing his hands through his greasy long hair and playing with his thick handle bar moustache.

"He needs a fix," said Nesta. Nesta was a no-nonsense agent, who had seen it all and could size up a junkie quicker than it would take for most people to decide whether to have cheese on their hamburger.

"Still, I don't think you're going to get anything out of this one," said Jack. "I've yet to break him."

"We'll see," said Nesta. "Ready?" he asked Angela.

"A confession a day keeps the doctor away," she retorted.

Angela and Nesta walked into the interrogation room, shut the door, and took a seat in the two metal chairs across the table from the big man, who was in a chair fixed to the floor.

"Felipe Corral," said Nesta, staring down the man with his steel grey eyes. Nesta never lost a stare down, because he never blinked.

"That's my name Chupas," he chuckled and added, "Don't wear it out!"

"My name is Special Agent Nesta from the Drug Enforcement Agency, and this is Angela Wollard from the FBI."

"Oh yeah?" He looked up and smirked. "Which one of you is the bad cop? The chick?"

"The 'chick' is *Agent* Wollard," said Nesta, firmly.

"Oh, so the Guera is the good cop and you must be the bad cop, huh Chupas?"

"We didn't come here to play games with you, Mr. Corral," said Angela, leaning forward across the table to look him straight in the eye.

"Then what did you come here for?" Corral laughed louder than his attitude. "So, you're both bad cops, huh Guera?" he asked, looking at Angela.

"Mr. Corral, we have you on assault with a deadly weapon and attempted murder..."

"Murder? What? I didn't touch that Guero! He attacked me!" Felipe pounded the table with his handcuffed fists, clenching his teeth.

"We're not talking about him," said Angela.

"The only way you're staying out of prison is to cooperate with us," said Nesta.

"Yo, you want me to rat on my brothers to you? A narc? You don't understand – they'll fuckin' kill me! You ain't got nothing anyways."

"We have video," said Angela.

"We were surfing. So you got a *surfing* video."

"What about the boats?"

"What about 'em?"

"We know what you were unloading."

"So what you need me for, Guera? You ain't got shit. That's why you're talking to me."

Angela left the room and came back with Jack, who took Angela's empty seat at the table.

"What's he doing here?" asked Felipe. "I thought you said he was dead."

"He needs to identify you," said Angela.

"Bullshit." Corral looked up at the ceiling.

"Mr. Corral, what do you know about Barbara Densmore?" asked Jack.

Corral looked at Jack with eyes and mouth wide open. "Who?"

"The president of the Orange Grove Homeowners Association."

Corral's hairy upper lip raised in disgust. "I don't got to talk to you, Chupas. I've had enough of this shit. I want to call my lawyer."

At that point, once Corral asked for a lawyer, the interview was over and Jack, Angela and Nesta left the room and joined Brent outside.

"He doesn't know anything about Densmore," Jack said.

"How do you know?" asked Nesta.

"Micro-expressions," said Brent. "Jack's an expert at them."

"Not only that," said Jack. "He really didn't know who Barbara Densmore was."

"That doesn't mean that one of the others doesn't know who killed her, or that they're not smuggling drugs," said Nesta. "I'll swear out a warrant and we'll turn their place upside down. We will, of course, share information with Agent Wollard."

"Thank you, Agent Nesta. I'm not sure how big of a help it will be. The trial has already started. But I appreciate it," said Brent.

CHAPTER TWENTY-EIGHT

Agents of the DEA and FBI surrounded the Orange Grove home of Keith Michel as Agent Nesta knocked on the door to serve the search warrant. Michel answered the door in his usual stupor, as if he had just gone to bed or just woken up from a long afternoon nap. Nesta served him the warrant and he looked at it, then back at Nesta with glassy eyes.

"Dude, this is harassment," protested Michel.

"Where are the other occupants of the residence?" asked Nesta.

"I'm the only one here," said Michel.

Nesta led the search team into the house and they immediately started trolling through everything.

"Are there any illegal drugs in the house?" Nesta asked Michel.

"Nope, only legal. I've got a prescription."

"I'm sure you do."

* * *

After two hours, the search team came up with nothing except Keith Michel's "medical marijuana." No guns – everything was clean.

"I'm going to sue you dude," Michel said to Nesta as he was walking out the door.

"Have a nice day," said Nesta. "I'll be back with arrest warrants for you and the rest of the Pep Boys."

* * *

The trial was underway. Nancy sat with Brent at counsel table, and her daughter Jillian sat in the front row behind her. There was nothing really for Jillian to do; just be there to support her mother.

"Mr. Chernow, you may call your first witness," said Judge Curtis.

"Thank you, Your Honor. I would like to call Joyce Bensley."

"Your Honor, may we approach?" asked Brent.

"Yes."

Once at the bench, Chernow started to complain. Brent could not understand the amount of emotion he had heaved into this trial.

"Your Honor," said Chernow, the defense is trying to derail the People's case."

"Excuse me, Your Honor, but isn't that my *job*? I can't sit here and let Mr. Chernow do whatever he wants. This is my client's life on the line."

"Okay, now knock it off, both of you," said Curtis. "What was your reason for the bench conference, Mr. Marks?"

"I anticipate that he is calling this witness to establish identity of the victim. We will stipulate that it was Barbara Densmore."

"Very well."

"Your Honor! The jury won't see the victim as a human being!"

"Alright, I will allow one question and one question only, after you have established the identity of your witness. Is that understood?"

"Yes, Your Honor."

When Brent got back to the bench, Nancy asked, "What was all that about?"

"He wants to get in before and after life and death photographs." Nancy grimaced.

As expected, Chernow identified the witness as Barbara Densmore's sister, and his one question was, "Ms. Bensley, I am showing you a photograph marked as Exhibit 1," said Chernow, panning the jury with the photograph as he approached the witness stand. "Can you identify this as a photograph of your sister, Barbara Densmore?"

"Yes, that's Barbara," said Bensley, putting a tissue to her eye and wiping out a tear.

All eyes of the jury were on the sister, and all 28 of them looked sad.

"Move Exhibit 1 into evidence, Your Honor."

"Objection, Your Honor, cumulative. Identity has already been established." It was a bad objection, given the last ruling, and Chernow was visibly upset. But, before he could speak, the judge ruled.

"Overruled, Mr. Marks."

Chernow next called the police photographer, so he could get in his dead photographs of Densmore.

"Objection, Your Honor, cumulative and prejudicial."

"Counsel approach," said the Judge.

"Your Honor, this is a death by poisoning case," argued Brent. "There are no injuries that can be shown from these photographs and their only purpose is to play the heartstrings of the jury. Their prejudicial effect outweighs any probative value."

"Mr. Chernow?"

"The photographs show the death of the victim, Your Honor."

"We will stipulate that she is deceased, Your Honor," said Brent.

"Your Honor, I must protest the constant petty objections of Mr. Marks. I should be able to present my case without him objecting to every question."

"With all due respect, Your Honor, it's not every question. And the defense has the right to object to anything we feel is improper."

"I will allow one photograph, and we're going to pick the least gruesome one," said Curtis, fanning them out like a deck of cards.

"This one. Agreed?" he asked, pointing to one of the photographs.

Chernow put the photographer on the stand, introduced the photograph, and it was allowed into evidence as People's Exhibit No. 2.

"Mr. Chernow, you may call your next witness.

"Thank you, Your Honor. I call Frances Templeton."

"Ms. Templeton, please stand in the witness box, face the clerk and be sworn," said the Judge.

Templeton walked up to the witness box, her eyes flashed to the Judge and then to the jury, and then she raised a semi-shaky right hand as instructed by the Clerk, took the oath, and then her seat.

"Ms. Templeton, you are the current president of the Orange Grove Homeowners Association, is that correct?"

"Yes, I am."

"And you became president of the Association upon the death of the victim, Barbara Densmore, is that correct?"

Templeton looked like a baby whose mother was force feeding her.

"Yes. I was the vice president before Barbara died."

"Ms. Templeton, did Mrs. Haskins fall behind in her homeowners association assessments last year?"

"Objection! Irrelevant!" Brent called out.

"Your Honor, It's foundational. I will connect it up," said Chernow, flashing a glare at Brent.

"Overruled."

Templeton testified that Nancy had fallen behind in her HOA assessments, and that the Association had initiated foreclosure on her home. Then came the real motive for murder.

"When Ms. Densmore was alive, did you witness any hostilities between the defendant, Mrs. Haskins and Ms. Densmore?"

"Well, yes I certainly did."

"Can you please describe these hostilities?"

"Well, Barbara was making her usual rounds, looking for violators of the Orange Grove regulations, and Haskins got into it with her."

"What do you mean by *got into it*?"

"Well, Barbara tried to give her a citation for an overgrown lawn and Haskins ran into her house, yelling, 'shove your ticket up your *you know what*,' and gave her the finger!"

"Move to strike as irrelevant, Your Honor."

"Mr. Chernow is establishing a foundation, Mr. Marks. I will allow it, subject to him connecting it up later," said Judge Curtis.

"Your Honor, if giving the finger is a motive for murder, then most everyone in this courtroom would be on trial," said Brent. A few people on the jury chuckled and smiled and there was laughter in the galley.

"Objection!" yelled Chernow. "Argumentative and improper!"

"The jury will disregard the question and Mr. Marks' comment," Judge Curtis said to the jury.

"Counsel, please approach the bench."

Brent knew the Judge was sharpening a hickory stick for him, and for just reason. He and Chernow approached the bench, out of earshot of the jury.

"Mr. Marks, I understand that it's difficult not to comment, but I allowed this evidence in as foundational and you know that your remark was not only argumentative, it was improper as well."

"Yes, Your Honor."

"Now please gentlemen, I've known you both for many years. You're both good lawyers. Don't compromise your ethics on this case."

Templeton then revealed that Nancy, on another occasion, told both her and Densmore that she wished them both dead. After a good deal more of irrelevant testimony, Brent was given the witness for cross examination.

"Ms. Templeton, you testified that foreclosure proceedings had been initiated on Mrs. Haskins' home by the HOA. Isn't it true that the very day before Ms. Densmore died the Court set aside those foreclosure proceedings?"

"Yes."

"So there were no more foreclosure proceedings on Mrs. Haskins' property at that point, is that correct?"

"Yes, but we were going to start them again."

"Move to strike after 'yes' Your Honor."

"Granted. Everything after 'yes' is stricken and the jury will disregard it."

"And when Mrs. Haskins 'gave the finger' to Ms. Densmore, that was about a year ago, wasn't it?"

"Well, yes, but…"

"Move to strike, Your Honor."

"Motion granted. The jury will disregard everything after 'yes'."

"And when she made the comment that she wished you were dead, it was even more than a year ago, isn't that correct?"

"Yes, it was."

"And in that one year period, you never heard about any other 'incident' between Ms. Densmore and Mrs. Haskins, isn't that correct?"

"That is correct," Templeton answered, reluctantly.

"In fact, besides the words you heard over a year ago, you're not aware of Mrs. Haskins ever taking any action to threaten the life of Ms. Densmore, are you?"

Frances frowned in frustration and said, "No, I suppose not."

"Move to strike as non-responsive and request that the witness be ordered to answer the question, Your Honor."

"The witness shall answer the question, if she can. It calls for a yes or no answer."

"No."

"Thank you, Ms. Templeton. You were at Barbara Densmore's home the night she died, weren't you?"

"Not before she died. After I heard about it, yes."

"And you got in using a key that Barbara had given you, is that correct?"

"Yes."

"You went there to go over the books and records of the Orange Grove Homeowners Association, is that correct?"

"To secure them."

"Ms. Templeton, it took you an awful long time to secure them, didn't it?"

"Objection, argumentative."

"Withdraw the question, Your Honor. You were at Ms. Densmore's home more than once that day, weren't you?"

"No, I was not."

Brent was drawing at straws, but maybe he could fish up some reasonable doubt for the jury by pointing to Templeton as a possible suspect. Templeton tightened her eyebrows and crossed her arms.

"Didn't you go there in the afternoon and come back at night because you forgot to get the books the first time you went over?"

"That's absurd."

"Answer the question please."

"No!"

"Didn't you go there the first time to clean up every trace of ricin?"

"No!"

"Objection, Your Honor," shouted Chernow.

"Sustained!" responded the Judge.

"And didn't you plant the ricin covered wrapping and flower food package in Mrs. Haskins' garage…"

"Your Honor!" objected Chernow.

"…which you accessed through the open side door?"

"No!" shouted Templeton.

"Objection sustained! Mr. Marks. The jury will disregard the last two questions and answers of this witness. Counsel, please approach."

After another good chewing out from the Judge, Brent said, "No further questions, Your Honor."

"Mr. Chernow?"

"No questions, Your Honor."

"Mr. Marks, do you anticipate calling Ms. Templeton during your case-in-chief?"

"I don't think so, Your Honor, but I don't want to close the door entirely, depending on what happens in Court."

"Do you have her under subpoena?"

"No, Your Honor."

"Very well. Ms. Templeton, you are excused. Mr. Marks may call you back, but at this time you are free to go, and the witness exclusion order no longer applies to you."

Chernow next called the EMTs who responded to the 911 call made by Barbara. They testified that they had found the victim in her office, on the floor, that she had a faint pulse and was not breathing. They tried to revive her, and kept up the attempts at CPR throughout her ride to the hospital in the ambulance, to no avail.

On cross examination, Brent had but one question for the lead EMT, a matter of fact, young looking fireman named Ted Clinton.

"Mr. Clinton, did you see any cut flowers when you were at the victim's residence?"

"Flowers?"

"Yes, flowers."

"No, we didn't see any flowers."

"Thank you. No further questions, Your Honor."

* * *

Brent stopped into the bathroom on the way out of the courtroom for the lunch break, and saw Bradley Chernow at one of the urinals.

"How's it hangin' Brad?" he asked, smiling, as he took a urinal on the same wall.

Chernow grimaced, zipped up his pants, hit the flush on the urinal, and turned to Brent and said, "The great Brent Marks. You think you're a super hot shit lawyer, don't you? You think because you kicked my ass in law school, this is going to be a walk around the block for you, huh?"

"What are you talking about Brad?"

"Mr. Chernow to you, Marks. You haven't tried a criminal case in what? Five years?"

"It's been a few years, yeah," said Brent, zipping up.

"Well I have news for you, Marks. Criminal law has changed a lot in the last five years and you're on *my* turf now."

"I doubt whether it's changed much in 250 years *Brad*," said Brent, washing his hands. "And whatever has changed, I can look it up," he said, ripping off a paper towel, drying off. "Do I think I can kick your ass? Is that what you're so emotional about? It's a promise!" he said, crumpling up the paper towel into a little ball and making a perfect basket in the trash can.

* * *

Brent dodged a few reporters who were gathered outside the Courthouse entrance on his way to meet Angela across the street at their usual café for the lunch break. In the middle of her salad, Angela popped the question that most lawyers dread hearing during a trial.

"So how's it going?"

"The trial?"

"Well, yeah, what else is going on *but* the trial?"

"Angela, asking a lawyer how the trial is going in the middle of it is like asking a husband if his wife is cheating on him. He's usually the last to know."

"Very funny."

CHAPTER TWENTY-NINE

"The People call Doctor Ignacio Perez."

Dr. Perez was sworn and took the witness stand. He faced the jury and "grandstanded" to them. Brent thought that it was only the second time he had seen Dr. Perez without a ham sandwich in his hand.

"Please state your name for the record."

"My name is Dr. Ignacio Perez."

"Dr. Perez, what is your current occupation?"

"I am a medical examiner for the county of Santa Barbara."

Perez spoke to the entire jury as if he were their personal physician, and he was explaining something to them about their medical examinations. He had a very calming bedside manner, which he used on the jury.

"Can you please summarize for the Court, your education and experience?"

"I am a certified medical examiner, currently serving with the County of Santa Barbara. I hold an M.D. and a PhD from Georgetown University School of Medicine, an A.B. from Dartmouth, and a medical license from the State of California, where I am board certified in clinical, anatomic and forensic pathology. I am a Diplomate of the American Board of Forensic Medicine, and I have worked as a Chief Medical Examiner for the County of Santa Barbara for the past 20 years."

"In how many trials have you testified, Doctor?"

"Not sure exactly. Over 50."

"Could you just give us a brief description of what forensic pathology is?"

"Yes, of course. Pathology, the larger field, is one of the medical specialties, and it has basically two subcategories; anatomic pathology and clinical pathology. Anatomic pathology deals with the study of disease. So it involves performing autopsies, looking at surgical specimens under a microscope, those kinds of things that the observer can actually see.

"Clinical pathology is performed in the laboratory, usually by clinical pathologists who head up a hospital laboratory and serve as consultants to hospital physicians in the interpretation of tests.

"Forensic pathology is a special area in pathology. The word forensic comes from the Latin word forum, which was the Roman courtroom. So, it is a type of pathology that is practiced by experts who clarify medical or scientific questions that come up in the courtroom. Most forensic pathologists work in a coroner's office or medical examiner's office and investigate sudden or unexpected deaths."

"How many autopsies have you done in your career, Doctor?"

"I've done many in the course of my career. Many hundreds."

Chernow had Perez disclose that he was being paid for his testimony, as part of his salary from the County, and that he had testified in both criminal and civil cases, for both the plaintiff and the defendant.

"Dr. Perez, please tell the jury what materials and reports you viewed in preparation for today's testimony."

"I reviewed my own autopsy report."

"Showing you a copy of People's Exhibit 1 and can you identify Exhibit 9 as your autopsy report?"

"Yes, that's my report."

"And, showing you what has been marked for identification as People's Exhibit 10, can you identify this document?"

"This is the death certificate for Barbara Densmore."

"Dr. Perez, as a result of your review, and your examination of the body, do you have an opinion within a reasonable degree of medical certainty what caused Barbara Densmore's death?

"Yes, I do."

"Objection, Your Honor, lack of foundation," Brent interjected.

"Sustained."

"Dr. Perez, would you please tell the jury the results of the autopsy?"

"As a result of my autopsy on the body of Ms. Densmore, I discovered fluid in her lungs and lesions in the trachea. Along with reported symptoms immediately before her death of coughing up white foam mixed with blood, it lead me to believe that she died from ricin poisoning."

The men on the jury looked queasy and nauseous from listening to the doctor's testimony. One of them appeared to be turning color.

"In this case, in my opinion, the ricin was inhaled, which explains the lesions in the trachea and fluid in the lungs. Inhalation of a dose of ricin the size of a few grains of salt is enough to kill an adult human being.

"Ricin is derived from the castor bean. Once in the body, it inhibits protein synthesis, causing cell death."

"Is there an objective test for ricin poisoning?"

"Yes, there is a urine test that can be performed by the Centers for Disease Control."

"Was that test performed in this case?"

"Yes. We drew a urine sample for testing and sent it to CDC. They are the only ones who do the testing. Since we knew that would take a long time to get the results, I also asked the police to examine the environment for the presence of ricin to confirm my diagnosis."

"Did you eliminate other possible causes of death?"

"Yes. I ran a full toxicology report on the victim's blood and also tested for influenza. Ricin symptoms can be similar to influenza. It also has symptoms that can be comparable to anthrax poisoning, so I ran blood tests which ruled that out."

"Are the results of that testing contained in Exhibit 11, the toxicology report?"

"Yes, they are."

"Your Honor, I move that People's Exhibits numbers 9, 10 and 11 be admitted into evidence."

"Objection to Exhibits 9 and 10, Your Honor. May we approach?"

Once at the bench, Brent objected to Exhibit 9, the autopsy report and Exhibit 10, the death certificate, on the grounds of lack of foundation, because it recited the cause of death as ricin poisoning, and that had not been established yet."

"Exhibit 11 will be admitted into evidence. The defense objection to Exhibits 9 and 10 is sustained, without prejudice."

"Dr. Perez, did you get the results back on the urine test?" asked Chernow.

"Yes, we did."

"What were the..."

"Objection, Your Honor, lack of foundation, hearsay, best evidence."

Chernow gave Brent a dirty look and he winked back at him. He was being a pest, it was true, but the results of the test had only recently been made available to both sides and neither Brent nor Jack had had the opportunity to question the chain of custody. Brent knew, of course, that the results were positive for ricin and that they would be allowed into evidence, but he threw out the objection "just in case."

"Counsel, please approach."

Brent hit the bench with his argument right away. "Your Honor, I haven't had the opportunity to interview the witness from CDC and neither has my investigator. We didn't have the test results at the time of the prelim, so the defense should be given the opportunity to question the witness from CDC before allowing the results to even be mentioned."

"He has a point, Mr. Chernow."

"Your Honor, the defense has been grandstanding for the jury since the beginning of this trial…."

"Excuse me, Your Honor, but this is a murder trial."

"Gentlemen, I've had just about enough of your bickering. I know it's a murder trial Mr. Marks. And Mr. Chernow, what is this whining all about? One would think the two of you were kids fighting in a sandbox. I'm going to sustain the objection, and let you recall Dr. Perez after you have established a foundation for the results, if you choose to do so."

Chernow limped back to the counsel table, went over his notes, and said, "Thank you, Your Honor, no further questions of this witness at this time, subject to our right to recall him."

"Cross examination?"

"Thank you, Your Honor."

"Dr. Perez, isn't it correct that the symptoms you observed; lesions on the trachea, blood mixed with foam in the mouth, and fluid in the lungs, are symptoms you may also expect to find with tracheal cancer?"

"Well I suppose you could, but it wasn't…"

"Thank you Doctor, move to strike after *could*, Your Honor."

"Granted. The jury is instructed that Dr. Perez' testimony stands at *Well I suppose you could.*"

"Couldn't you expect to find the same symptoms for lung cancer?"

"I suppose, but..."

"Move to strike *but*, Your Honor."

"Granted. The jury will disregard *but.*"

"And you didn't test to rule out tracheal cancer, did you?"

"No, I did not."

"And you didn't test to rule out lung cancer, did you?"

"No."

"Doctor, isn't pneumonia one of the most common diseases leading to death?"

"Yes."

"In fact, it is the sixth leading cause of death in the United States, isn't that correct?"

"I think so."

"Ricin poisoning, on the other hand, is very rare, isn't that correct?"

"Yes."

"Would you expect to see fluid in the lungs in cases of pneumonia?"

"Certainly."

"Wouldn't it also not surprise you to find a pneumonia patient coughing up blood?"

"That would not surprise me."

"And couldn't tracheal lesions be caused by excessive coughing?"

"Objection! Calls for speculation."

"Overruled. You may answer."

"Not these types of lesions."

"Move to strike as non-responsive, Your Honor."

"Denied."

"Thank you, Your Honor, no further questions," said Brent, turning over the witness to Bradley Chernow.

Chernow proceeded to rehabilitate Dr. Perez on redirect.

"Dr. Perez, has this urine test for ricin always been around?"

"No, it's relatively new."

"Is that why the CDC is the only facility who has it?"

"Objection, calls for speculation."

"Withdraw the question, Your Honor."

"Doctor, how long have you been aware that this urine test has been available?"

"A couple of years."

"And prior to that, what was the protocol to confirm ricin poisoning?"

"By finding an environmental sample."

"Which you did?"

"Yes, Detective Tomassi did."

"Dr. Perez, did you have any reason to suspect tracheal cancer?"

"No."

"Why not?"

"Because I examined the tissue of the trachea and did not see any abnormal cells. The types of symptoms that you're talking about would only present in advanced stages of tracheal cancer."

"What about lung cancer?"

"Same thing. The lung's cells are very delicate. I didn't find any tumors or evidence of abnormal cells in my examination."

"What about pneumonia?"

"Again, my examination did not indicate pneumonia. It was ricin poisoning, pure and simple."

* * *

"The People call Mr. Bennett Stevens."

Bennett Stevens stepped up to the clerk and was sworn, and took his place in the witness box. He was a young bureaucrat, about 30, slim and clean shaven, with cropped black hair and dark eyes.

"Mr. Stevens, do you work for the Center for Disease Control and Prevention in DeKalb County, Georgia?"

"Yes, I do."

"Can you please tell the jury what your position is at the Center for Disease Control?"

"I'm a senior lab technician."

"And what do your duties as a senior lab technician entail?"

"I handle laboratory tests for chronic diseases, environmental health threats and terrorism preparedness."

"Did you receive a urine sample from the Medical Examiner for the County of Santa Barbara for one Barbara Densmore?"

"Yes, we did."

"And the Medical Examiner asked for a test on the urine to detect the presence of ricin, is that correct?"

"Yes, the CDC has developed a test for measuring ricinine, which is a marker for ricin exposure."

"What did you do after you received the urine sample for testing?"

"We send out all our ricinine testing to a laboratory in our Laboratory Response Network. We have 32 laboratories in the United States who are certified biosafety level two and can perform this test."

Brent's ears perked up at this. It was screaming "chain of custody" all over the place. If there was any break in that chain of custody, if any facility who had handled the sample had not followed proper protocol, the results would not be admitted into evidence.

Chernow had the lab tech outline all the procedures for packaging, shipping and labeling the specimen, which, of course, had been properly performed by Dr. Perez himself. He went through the biosafety protocols ad nauseam. The jury was probably already lost by that time, and was fighting the boredom. A few jurors looked like they were day dreaming. A couple of others were nodding off. Then, when Chernow thought he had exhausted all possible objections, he asked, "And what were the results of the ricinine testing?"

"Objection, lack of foundation. Chain of custody, Your Honor," said Brent.

Chernow looked like he would hit the floor and pound his hands and feet against it in a temper tantrum.

"Your Honor, we've established a foundation."

"No he hasn't, Your Honor."

"Approach."

"Your Honor, we only have here one link in the chain," said Brent. "This gentleman from the CDC who seems to have captured the jury's full attention."

The Judge fought back a smile from the edges of his curled lips.

"Your Honor, we have established an unshakable foundation," Chernow argued.

"I'm not sure you have," said the Judge. We don't know how many hands the sample passed through when it left CDC. All we really know is what happened when it was delivered and when it came back."

"If it was the same sample, Your Honor," interjected Brent.

"Oh come on!" Chernow protested.

"We're almost at the end of the day," said the Judge. "We'll recess early to give you some time to do whatever you're going to do."

"Thank you, Your Honor," said Chernow, glaring at Brent, as if he wanted to stick his tongue out at him. Brent packed up his trial notebooks, putting them into a large rolling carrying case. The gallery had all but cleared out, except for one spectator. Sitting in the back row, Frances Templeton smiled at Nancy, Brent and Jillian as they walked out the door into a sea of reporters in the corridor.

CHAPTER THIRTY

Brent called Melinda from his cell phone right after court.

"Mims, better call Dr. Orozco and tell him to set aside next week to be called as an expert. Looks like we're gonna need him after all. See if you can get me an appointment with him."

"Okay boss, what about your messages?"

"I'll call you from home about those."

"Okay boss, I don't know quite how to say this, but Mrs. Haskins' case isn't really paying the bills now."

"I know, I know."

"Well, there's some new clients who want to see you."

"Set up appointments for tomorrow evening. There's no way I can do it tonight."

Brent's blood was racing with adrenalin as he drove home. The normal comforting effect of the harbor view as he descended Harbor Hills in his car was not as soothing as it usually was. Thoughts about the trial were coming at the speed of light; what did he do wrong, what was the next step? Other thoughts were coming at the speed of sound; feed the cat, check messages, check email, look at the trial notebook outlines for tomorrow, clean up, eat, get some rest.

As Brent was taking his cases out of the car, the adrenalin rush was still on, but it sneaked back a bit to reveal fatigue; not so much fatigue of the body, but of the mind. As he opened the front door, Calico, who was usually a blur of orange and white, snaking between his feet and making a beeline to the kitchen, was curled up in a ball on the windowsill. When he came in, she looked up at him, then put her head back down and slowly closed her eyes with disinterest.

"Hi honey!"

It was Angela! What a great surprise.

"Hey baby, I didn't expect to see you here."

"I knew you needed me. Now, don't worry about anything. I know you need to get at your emails and check with Melinda for your messages, so when you're ready, I've fixed a nice aperitif."

"Wow. That's almost enough to make me forget about my messages and the email."

Angela gave Brent a look with raised eyebrows that said "really?"

"Well, maybe not. I'll be right back."

Brent sailed through the emails with a renewed good feeling mood, responding to the most essential, erasing the junk mail, and saving the non-essential ones for a response later. Next – messages. He grabbed the phone.

"Hey Mimi."

"Boss, hi. Of course, everything is a crisis."

"Of course. I've been out of the office for two days."

Brent went over all the crises and gave instructions. All those wanting appointments were pushed until after the trial. Charles Stinson used to say, "During a trial, boy, you think, eat, sleep and crap only the trial." It was a statement that was not as wise as it was true.

When Brent came back into the great room, he saw the patio table flooded with the light of dozen candles, with the terrific harbor view in the background. He took a seat, and Angela poured him a deep red wine. He picked up the glass and savored the aroma.

"Argentinian Malbec," she purred.

They took some sips of wine and munched on Angela's hors d'oeuvres; little cheese eggplant things and assorted nuts and tasties. She put down her glass, went behind him and massaged his shoulders. *If this is what marriage is like, count me in!* he thought.

* * *

Jack's night was not as pleasant. He was, again, on the night shift. With his experience, Jack should have applied for a job with the Orange Grove Homeowners Association. He knew who was cheating on whom, who the alcoholics were, and, also, all the addicts. He even knew the local drug dealers, whom he kept a special eye on, waiting for them to screw up.

This time he had little presents for everyone, and it wasn't even Christmas. Just after Gary Goldstein pulled his car into his garage, Jack rang the bell and his wife, Jean, answered.

"Oh hello, Mr. Ruder!" she said, cheerfully.

Goldstein was grumbling in the background.

"Who's that at the door?"

"It's Mr. Ruder, dear."

He pushed her aside, albeit gently.

"What do you want?"

Jack smiled, and popped the subpoena into his hand.

"See you in court," he said, and walked away.

That would be the easiest one. He had stocked up enough junk food to make sure that, as soon as he spotted Keith Michel, he would have his little gift too, and so would fat Felipe, who had just made bail on the assault charge.

* * *

Brent and Angela dined on fabulous buttered lobster tails with zucchini parmesan, accompanied by a fine chilled French Sancerre. Angela let Brent cheat a little and go through his emails and trial notebooks while she did the dishes and drew him a special bath.

After a delicious bath, Angela treated Brent to an unbelievable massage.

"Angie, I'm in heaven, baby, but I feel so selfish. What can I do for you?"

"Funny you should ask that," she said, as she dropped her bathrobe and slipped under the sheets. "Why don't you use your imagination?"

CHAPTER THIRTY-ONE

The alarm bell on the phone struck like a hammer in Brent's head. He looked around. Angie wasn't there. Had it all been just a pleasant, crazy dream? Then he heard the shower running. She was already up. Time to face reality.

* * *

Chernow recalled the CDC witness, but it didn't do him any good. CDC's procedures had been followed carefully, as they were specially designed to guard against the release of contaminants that could be used in biological warfare or terrorism, but the loosely organized Laboratory Response Network turned out to be a way of passing the governmental buck, and its protocol did not comport with California's law on the chain of custody of evidence.

Chernow could not establish his chain of custody for the urine sample that had been tested positive for ricin, and it would never get to the jury. Brent, of course, was elated. But Chernow was ready to draw blood. He recalled Dr. Perez to the stand and emphasized that they had found an environmental sample of ricin in Orange Grove at Nancy's house, but they still could not explain the missing "puzzle pieces" of how no ricin was found in Barbara Densmore's home. Brent zeroed in on Perez for the kill.

"Dr. Perez, are you familiar with the term *clinical chemistry*?"

"Of course I am."

"Clinical chemistry is the process of analyzing bodily fluids, isn't that correct?"

"It is."

"Dr. Perez, is it true that the only way to clinically confirm a diagnosis of ricin poisoning is to test for the presence of ricin in the urine?"

"Clinical confirmation? Yes."

"And this test is only performed by the Centers for Disease Control?"

"Yes."

"So, you cannot clinically confirm, by the use of a test that was available to you, that the poison used on Mrs. Densmore was, in fact ricin, isn't that correct?"

Chernow said, "Objection, asked and answered," at the same time the doctor blurted out, "I know it was ricin."

"Move to strike, Your Honor, as non-responsive."

"Let me rule on the objection first. Yes, Mr. Chernow, it was asked and answered, but this is cross examination, so I will allow it," said Curtis. "The motion to strike is also granted, and the jury is instructed to disregard Dr. Perez' last answer. Dr. Perez, please answer the question."

"Could you repeat the question please?"

"Dr. Perez, you cannot clinically confirm, by the use of a test that was available to you, that the poison used on Mrs. Densmore was, in fact ricin, isn't that correct?"

Perez looked like he had just swallowed a piece of dog poop, but he had to respond, "Correct."

There were some gaping mouths in the jury box from that one. Nancy's eyes were bright, as she suppressed an expression of joy. Brent was making points. *I'd better not go back into the courthouse bathroom after court in case Brad wants another skirmish in front of the urinals,* he thought. The kill shot having been fired at Dr. Perez, he returned to finish off his victim.

"And you tested the clothes that Barbara Densmore was wearing the day of her death for ricin, isn't that correct?"

"Yes, it is."

"That test was negative, correct?"

"Correct."

"No ricin?"

"No ricin."

Brent was sure that the jury had no doubt that the urine sample tested positive for ricin, but the judge instructed them that no urine test was in evidence, and that they could not consider the testimony about it. It was a good win for Brent, but not enough to win the case. You could be sure that the jury would be thinking about the positive urine test when they deliberated, whether or not they discussed it amongst themselves.

Chernow's next witness was Detective Tomassi, whom Brent knew he could not crack on cross examination, but that the man would, according to Jack, respond truthfully to a properly framed question. Chernow walked Tomassi through his assignment and work experience, and his discovery of the wrapping and flower food packet at Nancy's house. Brent scanned the juror's faces during the testimony. All seemed to be expressing their belief in Tomassi's veracity. Brent had to be clever with how to spin this.

"Detective Tomassi," Chernow asked, "Where did you find the cellophane wrapping, marked as People's Exhibit No. 12 and flower food packet, marked as People's Exhibit No. 13?"

"In the defendant's garage."

"Detective, why was the discovery of cellophane wrapping and flower food important to you?" asked Chernow.

"It was a material that is normally used to wrap flowers purchased or delivered from a flower store. We knew that a similar flower food had been found in a kitchen drawer at the victim's house, and we were looking for a powdery substance that could have easily been hidden in such a packet."

"Showing you what has been marked for identification as People's Exhibit 14, can you identify this as the flower food package found in the victim's home?"

"Yes."

"But you didn't find any flowers?"

"Correct."

"What did you do with the cellophane wrapping when you found it?"

"I placed it in a plastic evidence bag, booked it in as evidence, and delivered it to the forensic lab for fingerprint and toxicology analysis."

"And, subject to my witnesses being called on this matter, Your Honor, Detective, did you receive a report back from forensics?"

"Yes, I received a fingerprint analysis report and a toxicology report."

"Showing you what has been marked for identification as People's Exhibit numbers 15 and 16, can you identify these as the fingerprint and toxicology reports?"

"Yes."

"And what did you learn from these reports?"

"That the cellophane contained traces of ricin and that Barbara Densmore's fingerprints were on the wrapping."

Two of the women on the jury let out a surprised sigh. Chernow continued.

"Your Honor, I move that Exhibits 13 through 16 be admitted into evidence."

"Objection?"

"No objection as to 13 and 14, Your Honor, but I object to the reports – Exhibits 15 and 16 for lack of foundation."

"Exhibits 13 and 14 are received. Mr. Chernow, you will need to authenticate the reports."

"Yes, Your Honor. No further questions."

"Mr. Marks?"

"Thank you, Your Honor. Detective Tomassi, isn't it true that the forensic team you described made a thorough search of Barbara Densmore's residence for evidence?"

"Yes, sir."

"And you specifically instructed them that you were looking for some type of poison, isn't that correct?"

"Yes, sir."

"And isn't it also correct that, all the interviews of witnesses that you have conducted indicated that Barbara was at home all day before being taken to the hospital in the ambulance?"

"That is correct, sir."

"So there is no doubt in your mind that she would have ingested the poison at her residence, isn't that correct?"

"Objection, calls for speculation," Chernow interjected.

"He can answer if he has an opinion," said the Judge. "Detective Tomassi, answer the question if you can."

"No, sir, there is no doubt in my mind that it occurred at her residence."

"Is it also true that, at her residence, your forensic team found no traces of ricin?"

"Yes, that is true."

"And they also found no traces of any poison of any kind, isn't that correct?"

"Yes, that is correct."

"You testified, Detective Tomassi that, as a result of a search of Mrs. Haskins' house that you did find cellophane wrapping in her garbage can with traces of ricin on it, is that correct?"

"Yes, that is correct."

"And this cellophane wrapping had no fingerprints on it besides the victim's, Barbara Densmore, isn't that correct?"

"That is correct."

"This means that, if anyone had wiped the cellophane clean, they would have done so only before Barbara Densmore handled it, isn't that correct?"

"Objection, calls for speculation," said Chernow.

"Sustained. The jury will disregard the question."

"You didn't find any flowers at Mrs. Haskins' residence, did you Detective?"

"No."

"And you found no evidence of any ricin or ricin manufacture at her home, did you?"

"Besides the flower wrapping and flower food, no."

"And you were careful not to handle the wrapping, putting it in an evidence bag and booking it as evidence because of your procedures in handling evidence, isn't that correct?"

"Yes, and because of the potentially dangerous toxins we were looking for."

"You follow these procedures to make sure there is no evidence tampering or contamination, isn't that correct?"

"Yes, that's correct."

"Isn't there a procedure to contain a crime scene as well?"

"Yes, there is."

"That's why we see on TV the police putting up yellow tape, right?"

Several members of the jury chuckled.

"That's right."

"The procedure is to make sure that no potential evidence at a crime scene is tampered with or contaminated, right?"

"Right."

"And, when you are investigating a crime scene, nobody but Sheriff's personnel are allowed at the scene, to make sure none of the potential evidence is compromised, correct?"

"That's correct."

"You were the first officer to arrive on the scene the night of Barbara Densmore's death, weren't you?"

"Yes."

"And your team put up that yellow tape in front of her house, just like on TV, didn't they?"

"Yes."

"To keep people out, correct?"

"Yes."

"But when you arrived, there was someone else already inside Ms. Densmore's residence, wasn't there?"

"Yes, Frances Templeton was there."

"You detained her at gunpoint, didn't you?"

"Yes, I did, until I was convinced that she wasn't a threat to my safety."

"How did Ms. Templeton get into Barbara Densmore's house?"

"She had a key."

* * *

Chernow next called a virtual parade of police officers as witnesses, who testified how they had secured the crime scene, and the forensic team who had combed Densmore's house for evidence. Brent put them through a cursory cross examination, but most of them had really nothing to add to the case, and certainly nothing damaging.

Then he called Dr. Fernando Medina, a poison expert, whom Brent agreed was qualified to testify. Medina looked like he had been born to be a scientist, as if he were more comfortable with a test tube in his hand than by his side or in his pocket. He was clean cut, average looking, with plain brown hair and plainer brown eyes.

"Dr. Medina, how exactly is ricin made?"

Although introverted and lacking in social skills, Dr. Medina spoke to the jury in a very non-technical manner that made it easy for the jurors to understand.

"Without going into the actual technicalities of it, it is made from the castor bean. After the beans are put into an oil press to extract castor oil, the "cake," or crushed part of the beans that is left over is pounded into a powder, which contains ricin, and is lethal unless put through an autoclave."

"Are castor beans difficult to come by?"

"Why no. Anyone can buy castor beans from just about any seed dealer."

"And is it difficult to pound the leftover bean mash into a powder?"

"Not at all. Anyone can do that as well. You just have to wear protective clothing like gloves and a protective mask; the type they have in any high school science class."

Brent barreled ahead on cross examination. "Dr. Medina, you say that anyone can make ricin, is that correct?"

"Yes, anyone can."

"Isn't it true that you have to possess a degree of scientific knowledge in chemistry to refine the ricin powder?"

"Actually no. After ten minutes of Internet research, anyone with a computer can learn how to make ricin. And, as I said before, the beans are easy to come by and there's no special equipment required besides an oil press and protective clothing."

"Move to strike after 'no' Your Honor."

"Denied."

It turned out to be a terrible mistake, the classic one that lawyers are taught in law school never to make. Never ask a question that you do not know the answer to; especially of an expert.

Chernow next called Thomas Benton, who was qualified to testify as a forensics expert, and described, with the aid of computer modeling, how the flower food package containing ricin in the bouquet was rigged to explode and distribute its poisonous payload to the unsuspecting victim who unwrapped the flower package.

Benton had big, curious hazel eyes, as if he was always on the lookout for a new discovery. He had a few hours' worth of grey stubble on his chin that gave away his age and the fact that he colored his dark brown hair.

"Mr. Benton, can you explain the expertise that was required to rig this package to explode?"

"There was no expertise required at all. It was a very crude device. The perpetrator simply used an empty flower food package, filled it with ricin, using protective clothing I assume, and taped it to the plastic wrapping here," he said, pointing to his computer model diagram on the screen. "When the cellophane was ripped open, the package would naturally empty its contents. Being a fine powder, it would naturally become airborne."

Brent made his points here in cross examination.

"If the package was rigged to explode as you described, isn't it true that the powder would have been distributed over a large area?"

"Normally, yes."

"And you would expect at the death scene there would be traces of powder on the floor and on the victim's clothes, would you not?"

"You would, yes, unless somebody had cleaned it up."

"Interesting you should mention that because, if somebody had cleaned it up with, for example, a vacuum cleaner, wouldn't you expect to find traces of the powder left on the floor?"

"Yes, unless it had also been washed."

"And wouldn't you expect to find the powder in the vacuum cleaner bag and apparatus?"

"Yes, unless of course, that had also been thoroughly cleaned."

"So, unless the site of the explosion had been meticulously washed, you would expect to find some traces of ricin, isn't that correct?"

"Yes."

Chernow next called Thomas Finlay, the fingerprint expert, who looked at the jury with squinty ashen eyes through thick glasses, as if he had already worn them out looking at too many fingerprints. Finlay testified that the fingerprints on the wrapper matched those of Barbara Densmore's. On cross examination, he admitted, matter-of-factly, that there no fingerprints of Nancy's found on the wrap, or anyone else's besides Densmore's.

The minutes clicked on into the hours, and the jury, once alert and attentive, looked really worn down. Finally, the Judge adjourned for the day. And sure enough, Brent noticed upon leaving that Frances Templeton was there, in what had surely become her season ticket seat.

Brent resisted the temptation to get a free commercial or two from the TV crews that accosted him outside the Courthouse. There would be plenty of time for that after the trial.

CHAPTER THIRTY-TWO

There would be no gourmet dinners tonight, no baths, no romantic interludes, only the fantastic harbor view, the patio, and various alcoholic libations. Brent and Jack had to get together for a brainstorming and preparation session because the next court day, Bradley Chernow was expected to rest his case. Then it would be Brent's turn.

On the way home, Brent stopped at Dr. Orozco's office to brief him on the next days' testimony. Dr. Jaime Orozco was a medical examiner that Brent had worked with before, on one of his most important cases. He was smart and sharp, and had a great bedside manner; he just wasn't very presentable. Brent had the impression that he had attended the same sandwich eating autopsy school that Dr. Perez had gone to. Nevertheless, he was the best and he was Brent's next witness.

Brent's minor victory in getting the urine sample suppressed could be a pyrrhic victory. After all, the jury knew full well that the test had come back positive for ricin, they just technically couldn't consider it. Orozco would brief the jury as to the other medical conditions which could generate the same symptoms. His contradictory testimony alone may be enough for the jury to question Dr. Perez' testimony.

* * *

"Jack, please don't say you have good news and bad news," Brent said, as he sipped on a Baileys on the rocks and watched the moon rise above the Santa Barbara harbor.

"I won't. It's all bad."

"Even better. Those flowers didn't just get up and walk away. And the cellophane wrapping didn't transport itself to Nancy's garage by magic. Someone wearing gloves put it there after they had thoroughly ridden every grain of ricin from Densmore's home. It was either Nancy, which I doubt, or someone trying to frame her."

"And that someone may or may not be the real killer."

"Exactly. Great minds do think alike."

"Well, in the reasonable doubt corner, we have the People's witness, Frances Templeton, who is a lying sack of shit, but I can't find anything tying her to the flowers."

"And nothing on the flower shop?"

"Nobody knows where they came from. I covered every shop within a five mile radius."

"Maybe you should try a ten mile radius. What about her whereabouts between the time the ambulance arrived and the time the detective arrived?"

Jack took gulpful of beer from the bottle. "She's got an alibi."

"Since when does a witness for the prosecution need an alibi?"

"Since the defense is investigating her. She was with a friend. All that day and, after the police released her, all night."

"I suppose you talked to this friend?"

"Yes, and as alibis go, it's about standard."

"Nothing I can rip a hole in?"

"I'm afraid not. She's pretty credible."

"Okay, so she can account for her whereabouts. What else have we got?"

"Gary Goldstein, whom I've served with subpoena. But I think he's just a guy with anger issues."

"Anger issues are good for us. What about the drug dealers?"

"I've served Michel and Corral, but neither one is talking."

"What about the DEA investigation? Corral won't even talk to the U.S. Attorney to save his own butt?"

"He says that the Colombians will kill him and his entire family if he does, so he's willing to do the time."

"What about Keith Michel?"

"They're still investigating. Never found the marijuana that was smuggled in, if that's what it was. So now they're trying to get someone on the inside who knows them to wear a wire."

Brent spent the evening going over Jack's reports, working out questions for Michel, Corral and Goldstein. He also did a post-mortem on the day in court in anticipation of what appeared to be the next and last day of the prosecution's case-in-chief. Sometime during that, he had nodded off. He awoke to Calico, nudging him and purring. She was telling him it was time to go to bed.

CHAPTER THIRTY-THREE

Chernow next put on Dr. Gerald Gregory, a poison expert, who looked like the only thing he had ever worn was a lab coat. In fact, his beige two piece cotton suit looked like it had been made from a lab coat or designed after one, because it was so long. His tie was loosely affixed to the collar because of his lack of a neck. It was as if his shoulders were attached directly to his head. Gregory had a squirmy face, darting eyes and a moustache that looked like one of those fuzzy caterpillars.

He explained how lethally toxic ricin was. Less than 1.8 mg could kill the average adult human. It killed by inhibiting protein synthesis, which was the reason why symptoms often took hours or even a day to appear. And it was difficult, if not impossible to detect after ingestion, all of which made it the perfect poison. It also was very rare; not the type of poison you would find in the garden section at Home Depot. If you had ricin, there was only one reason for it, and that was to kill another (or more than one other) human being.

Brent had no questions on cross examination. Chernow had now laid out all the pieces of his puzzle for the jury, except for the urine test.

"Your Honor, the People rest," he declared.

"Mr. Marks, is the defense ready?"

"Yes, Your Honor."

"You may call your first witness."

"I call Jack Ruder."

Jack did not disappoint. He wore a crisp, grey G-man suit and looked more like a witness for the prosecution than the defense.

"Mr. Ruder, what is your occupation?"

"I am a California licensed private investigator."

"And can you please tell the jury a little about your background and experience?"

Jack turned to the jury, just as he had rehearsed it with Brent, and spoke to them as if he were hosting them at a dinner party in his home. However, he couldn't shake the military-type cop talk that he had been using for years, especially in the courtroom.

"I hold Bachelor's and Master's Degrees in Criminology from California State University Long Beach. After leaving CSULB, I worked for about five years as a police officer for the LAPD. Then I worked for 21 years for the Federal Bureau of Investigation, Los Angeles office, the last ten of those in the Violent Crime Division, where I served on several serial killer task forces, including the Night Stalker case."

"Showing you what has been marked for identification as Defense Exhibit A, can you identify this document?"

"Yes, that is my resume."

"Your Honor, I move that Defense Exhibit A be admitted into evidence."

"Objection?"

Chernow's lips pursed and the Judge paused. He looked like he was finishing a bite of food or something.

"No objection, Your Honor," he finally conceded.

"Exhibit A is received."

"You were hired by the defense in this case, is that correct?"

"Yes."

"And you are being paid for your services?"

"Yes."

"What was your assignment in this case?"

"To investigate the death of Ms. Barbara Densmore."

Jack told the jury, albeit in his cop-like jargon, of his interviews with the Goldstein's, Keith Michel and Frances Templeton, but when he told about the stakeout of Keith Michel's house, this is where Chernow sought to get even with the objections.

"Objection, Your Honor," said Chernow, savoring every word of his argument. "This is irrelevant, immaterial, and highly prejudicial to the People's case."

"Counsel please approach."

At the bench, Chernow couldn't stop hurling objections. Finally, Brent interrupted.

"Your Honor, may I be heard please?"

"Yes, Mr. Marks."

"Your Honor, this witness is necessary to lay a foundation for half of the witnesses on my witness list. Whether or not this raises reasonable doubt as to my client's guilt is for the jury to decide. However, just as the People were allowed to connect up their foundational evidence, I would ask for the same indulgence from the Court."

"I'm going to allow it," said the Judge. Chernow looked like a little kid whose dad had taken a lollipop away from him.

Jack described the stake out, the ensuing shoot out and chase, and the subsequent arrest of Felipe Corral on suspicion of drug smuggling and assault. Then he was prompted to describe his investigation of Gary Goldstein.

"Objection, Your Honor. This has gone far beyond foundational and is definitely prejudicial to the People's case, not to mention irrelevant and immaterial."

Then don't mention it, thought Brent.

After another lengthy bench conference, the Judge declared, "Overruled, I will allow it."

Finally, Jack left the witness stand unscathed, having paved the way for the "suspects" to come.

And they came. First to testify was Gary Goldstein, who had been sitting in the gallery fuming, looking like he had a severe case of indigestion, and an even stronger case of impatience. He was with his lawyer, Richard Hannaford, an octogenarian attorney whose reputation and experience were almost as big as his nose. He was one of the most respected criminal attorneys in Santa Barbara. Brent did not expect the testimony to last long. Hannaford sat at the defense counsel table with Brent. He couldn't bear the thought of sharing a table with the prosecution, having never been on that side of the courtroom. It would be like a fish swimming in tomato juice.

"Mr. Goldstein, you reside in the Orange Grove townhome development at 4440 Orange, is that correct?" Brent asked.

"Yes, I do."

"And you are here because the defense served you with a subpoena, isn't that correct?"

"Yeah, your investigator, Jack Ruder did."

"Mr. Goldstein, did you know the victim, Barbara Densmore?"

"Yes, she was the president of the Homeowners Association."

"Isn't it true that, during her tenure as president, you had several altercations with her?"

"Your Honor," said Hannaford, who stood up, cleared his throat, and put one hand in his pocket. With those two words, the jury was locked on Hannaford like he was E.F. Hutton, and so was the Judge.

"Your Honor," he repeated, "While, of course, Mr. Goldstein respects this Court and is here in full compliance with the subpoena, after due consultation with counsel, and an abundance of caution, he has decided to exercise his Fifth Amendment Privilege against self-incrimination."

Anyone who has ever seen a police detective movie has heard the line, "you have the right to remain silent." This was that right in action, and it was more of a gift to Brent than Goldstein's testimony would have been. The jury had no idea what trouble went on between Goldstein and Densmore and never would. But that would not keep them from speculating what it was, and now they had another possible guilty party they could point the finger at.

Not only that, Nancy would *not* be exercising her right to remain silent. As much as the jury could be instructed not to hold a defendant's silence against them, that it did not constitute an admission of anything, and that the People were the only ones obligated to prove *anything* in the case, just the fact of Nancy speaking would weigh in on the reasonable doubt scale in her favor for the jury, unless, of course, she was destroyed on cross examination. The only regret Brent had was that he would not get to listen to the old man's cross examination. He was a legend.

Brent next called Felipe Corral to the stand. The jury had been prepared for his testimony by Jack Ruder, and it was a good thing because his attorney, Martin Katzenberg, a short little guy with a belly, graying hair and matching glasses, interposed his objection right away.

"Your Honor, Mr. Corral exercises his Fifth Amendment privilege against self-incrimination."

"Very well, Mr. Katzenberg. Mr. Corral, you are excused."

"Your Honor, the defense calls Keith Michel."

Surf was up. Michel walked into court in a suit, with combed hair. He looked like a teenager at a relative's wedding. With him was a lawyer that Brent did not recognize. At this point, Chernow had another fit. "Your Honor, may counsel approach the bench?" he asked, as if out of the blue.

"Your Honor, this is highly prejudicial," said Chernow. "The defense is calling witnesses he knows full well will take the Fifth because of various *other* criminal activities, and the jury is drawing the inference that they may be guilty parties implicated in this murder. I move for the exclusion of Keith Michel as a witness."

"Mr. Marks?"

"Your Honor, they may be guilty parties implicated in this murder. As I understand it, the DEA and FBI are investigating Mr. Corral and Mr. Michel about their possible involvement. It would be malpractice for me not to call them as witnesses."

"Mr. Marks, I see your point, but I also see the People's point. I suggest you inquire of Mr. Michel's attorney if he intends to take the Fifth as well, because I'm not going to have you line up possible guilty parties who have nothing to say to the jury to try to rack up points."

"Yes, Your Honor."

"If he's taking the Fifth, he will be excluded."

"Yes, Your Honor."

"Thank you, Your Honor," said Chernow, gloating.

It was no surprise that Keith Michel's attorney would be taking the Fifth, so the parade of suspects came to an end, as did the day. The last one to leave, as usual, was Frances Templeton, who smiled at Brent, Nancy and Jillian as they walked by.

"Why does that woman come here every day?" asked Nancy.

"Maybe she has nothing better to do. Or maybe she has a morbid desire to see something bad happen to you."

CHAPTER THIRTY-FOUR

Brent was on the home stretch. He fully expected that he would rest his case the following day, and that the last day would be reserved for final argument, unless Chernow had any rebuttal witnesses. He spent a couple of hours with Nancy in his office, going over her testimony.

"Well, Nancy," said Brent, "This is it. How do you feel about it?"

"Honestly Brent, I'm so nervous I don't even think I can say my own name." Her hands were trembling. "What do I do?"

Brent put his hand on top of hers and said softly, "First, calm down. There's only one thing you can do, Nancy. You know how to do it and it will get you out of any jam in cross examination."

"What's that?" asked Nancy, wide-eyed and pensive.

"Just tell the truth. You know the old adage, *the truth will set you free.* Well, in your case, it will. If you tell your story, and tell it like you first told it to me, then you'll be fine." She looked like she had calmed down.

"Okay Brent. I trust you."

"Trust yourself, Nancy. I know you've heard yourself tell your story a million times, but you know what the best thing about the truth is?"

"What?"

"You don't have to remember what you said."

Nancy smiled relief.

"Just a few ground rules," said Brent. "Before you answer a question, make sure you understand it. If you don't, say you don't understand the question. That way you won't be tricked. If you don't remember something, say you don't remember."

"Alright, Brent. I will."

"Good. Now let's go over one more time all the possible questions I can think of on cross."

* * *

Brent had no dinner plans for tonight. Just himself, the cat, and his final argument. He polished the outline, knowing that he would look at it for the first ten minutes and then the rest of it would come naturally. He wasn't one to practice in front of a mirror or anything like that. He could hear it in his head.

CHAPTER THIRTY-FIVE

The gallery was packed with spectators, so many that the Fire Marshal had to order some of them to leave. The courtroom had runneth over with them. Word of the trial had spread through the newspapers and television, and there were more lookie-loos than Brent had ever experienced in a trial.

"Please call your first witness, Mr. Marks."

"Thank you, Your Honor. I call Dr. Jaime Orozco.

Dr. Orozco rolled up to the stand in his ancient, out-of-style suit with a rumpled tie, and his belly hanging over the belt line. He looked like big bear. Despite his slightly unkempt appearance and scraggly small beard, which he felt made him look more "distinguished," once Orozco made eye contact with the jury Brent could see they felt comfortable with the old guy.

"Dr. Orozco, what is your profession?"

"I am a private medical examiner."

"Can you please summarize for the jury, your background, education and experience?"

"Yes. I have over 30 years' experience as a pathologist and medical examiner. I hold an MD, a PhD, and a medical license in the state of California, where I am board certified in clinical, anatomic and forensic pathology. I also have a JD from Southwestern Law School and am a licensed attorney in California and New York. I am a Diplomate of the American Board of Pathology. I worked as a Chief Medical Examiner for the County of Los Angeles for ten years and another 10 years for the Federal Bureau of Investigation."

"Have you testified as an expert witness in trials before?"

"Many times."

"How many times?"

"Too many to count, I'm afraid. I would have to say tens, maybe even hundreds of trials."

"How many autopsies have you done throughout your career, Doctor?"

"Too many to count. I would say many hundreds, maybe even into the thousands."

As Bradley Chernow had done with Dr. Perez, Brent had Dr. Orozco reveal that he was working for money, and that he had testified for the plaintiff's and the defendant's sides in many criminal and civil cases. His curriculum vitae was marked for identification and admitted as a defense exhibit.

"Dr. Orozco, please tell the jury what materials and reports you reviewed in preparation for today's testimony."

Dr. Orozco did just that. He talked to the jury as if they were in his living room, and they were all seated in front of the fireplace, listening to stories.

"I reviewed the autopsy report of Dr. Perez and the toxicology report."

"Did you have the ability to do your own autopsy on the victim?"

"Unfortunately, no. The victim's body had been cremated at the point I was brought into the case."

"Dr. Orozco, if you had been able to do your own autopsy, what would you have done differently than was described in Dr. Perez' report?"

"Objection, calls for speculation," Chernow chimed in.

"Expert hypothetical, Your Honor."

"Overruled. It is in the nature of an expert hypothetical question, in reverse manner," said the Judge. "You may answer, Doctor."

"I would have tested tissue samples for abnormal pathology such as cancer cells. I would have tested the tissues for infectious bacteria."

"Didn't you perform these tests on tissue samples that had been saved from the autopsy?"

"Yes, some tissue samples were made available to me, but not enough to make comprehensive tests that could result in any conclusions."

"Dr. Orozco, as a result of your review, do you have an opinion within a reasonable degree of medical certainty what caused Ms. Densmore's death?

"Yes, I do."

"Would you please tell the jury your opinion?"

"In my opinion, Ms. Densmore's death was caused by acute respiratory failure."

"Is that consistent with ricin poisoning?"

"It could be, but there was no indication from Dr. Perez' report besides his conclusion that ricin was to blame. Absolutely no pathological evidence at all. It could have been any number of other factors which caused her respiratory system to shut down, according to the medical history and forensic evidence."

"Such as what?"

"Tracheal or lung cancer, for one. Common pneumonia for another. Unless I had found ricin on her clothes or in the immediate vicinity of the death scene, there is no way I could conclusively determine that it was ricin poisoning."

"No further questions, your honor."

"Cross?"

"Thank you, your honor," said Chernow.

"Dr. Orozco, wouldn't your opinion be different if you knew that an environmental sample of ricin were found?"

"That depends on the environmental sample. Certainly, if the deceased were found dead and there was ricin in the immediate environment, yes."

"And, you did not examine the body?"

"That's what I said."

"So then, your opinion is based on pure speculation, isn't it Doctor?"

"Objection, Your Honor, argumentative."

"It is argumentative, but I will allow the answer."

"No. My opinion is based on the reports. I didn't have to speculate about anything," said Dr. Orozco, innocently.

"No further questions, Your Honor."

"Mr. Marks?"

"Nothing further, Your Honor."

"Then we will break for the afternoon recess and resume at 1:30.

* * *

For a change of scene, Brent met Angela for lunch at The Gallery Café. It was always a pleasant retreat to pass through the art gallery first and admire all the new arrivals, before exiting to the dining area in the beautiful stone courtyard. Angela sat in the corner, behind the fountain. Among the flowers bursting from the vine covered stone walls and the magnificent orchids, her beauty stood out above all the rest.

"So, you're on the home stretch?" she asked.

"I figure one more day."

"Any chance you can join me tonight?"

"I can't go out or anything."

"I know. I thought I would come over."

"I'd love to have you, but I'll be preparing."

"Not the whole night."

Brent smiled, as he thought to himself how lucky it was that fate put this woman right in his path. She was truly the nicest person he had ever known. He raised his glass of red wine to her, and said, "Angela, you are by far the most wonderful person I have ever met, not to mention the most beautiful. Here is to you, and my incredible luck for having met you."

Angela's cheeks flushed, and she smiled.

"Where did that come from?"

"From my heart."

Brent and Angela spent an hour in this lovely oasis, and almost didn't notice that the time had passed and it was time to come back to reality.

CHAPTER THIRTY-SIX

Back in the tightly filled courtroom, all eyes were on Nancy as she took the stand in her own defense. Brent saw that the reporters in the gallery were at ready position, with their steno books open and pencils sharpened.

"Mrs. Haskins, are you are aware that you have a Fifth Amendment privilege against self-incrimination, and that you do not have to testify in this case?"

"Yes."

"And you realize that the People have the burden to prove guilt beyond a reasonable doubt, that you have no obligation to do or say anything, and that, by giving up your right to remain silent, you are waiving that right?"

"Objection compound," said Chernow, interrupting the drama that the jury was fixed on.

"I'll allow it," said the Judge.

"I have nothing to hide," said Nancy, looking at the jury. "I'm innocent," she exclaimed, with an affirming nod.

"Mrs. Haskins, did you like Ms. Densmore as a person?"

"No, I didn't care for her at all. That's no secret. Oh, but I didn't kill her," she added, raising a few smiles from the men on the jury.

"Move to strike the last sentence, Your Honor," objected Chernow.

"Denied. Please continue, Mr. Marks."

"Why didn't you like her, Mrs. Haskins?"

"Well, I understand that the Homeowners Association has a right to collect their money. And I understand that they can use foreclosure in certain circumstances."

Nancy looked at the jury. The older folks seemed to empathize with her, by the looks on their faces.

"But Barbara was never *human* about it. She never considered that this was my *home,* and never gave me a chance to try to work things out. All she wanted to do was to take my house."

"Did the Homeowners Association take your house?"

"No, you stopped them in court," she said proudly, a nice testimonial for Brent's lawyering skills.

"So, after you stopped the foreclosure in court, you had no further need to fight with the Homeowners Association, did you?"

"No, I didn't. All I had to do was come up with a payment plan."

"Your Honor, I ask that the Court take judicial notice of the order of the Superior Court in the case of *Haskins v. Orange Grove Homeowners Association*, and that it be admitted into evidence as Defense Exhibit C."

"No objection? It is received."

"And I would like Your Honor to note that the order halting the foreclosure was granted one day *before* Barbara Densmore's death."

"So noted."

"Mrs. Haskins, can you describe the incident where you told Ms. Densmore to "shove" her ticket?"

"That's embarrassing, Brent." Nancy's cheeks turned pink, even though they had gone over it before.

"Please, explain to the jury what happened."

Nancy sighed and took a deep breath.

"Well, that day was a terrible one for me. My husband had just recently died and I was sad, upset and lonely. I saw Barbara writing out one of her tickets for something – they always write out tickets for everything – if your lawn is not mowed good enough, if your trash cans aren't taken back into the garage soon enough – you name it, they have a ticket for it," she said to the jury, with a stern look.

"Anyway, Barbara came running up to me, waving that ticket and I tell you I didn't want any part of it. And I got so mad, well, you know what I said," she exclaimed, turning a little redder.

"Can you explain why you told Barbara Densmore and Frances Templeton that you wished them dead?"

"I think everyone has said that at one time or another. I didn't mean it!"

"Then, why did you say it?"

"They just made me so upset, I didn't know what else to say. I could never hurt anyone, no matter what! You have to believe me!" she implored, looking at the jury with wounded eyes.

"Did you have any personal problems with Barbara?"

"Oh, heavens no!" said Nancy, looking right in at the jurors. "It was just that darn homeowners association I had problems with. If it wasn't Barbara, it would have been someone else. We had others before her and they were just as bad."

"Mrs. Haskins, did you kill Barbara Densmore?"

"No, Brent, I swear as God is my witness I didn't. And I'm so afraid from this whole thing." Tears rolled down Nancy's cheeks, and the women on the jury all looked like they were going to cry with her. "I'm sorry," she sobbed, "I just can't imagine that anyone would even think such a thing, let alone actually accuse me of murder!"

Brent paused and looked at the jury. From his point of view, they all looked as if they imagined Nancy in her kitchen, baking cookies, instead of concocting poisonous booby traps and putting them in flower bouquets.

Chernow was so eager to cross examine Nancy, it seemed as if he would pee his pants. He was wiggling in his chair and biting on the top of his pen the entire time, in between making furious notes.

"Your Honor, is it about time for the afternoon break?" Brent asked. "It looks like it may be time for a bathroom break," he added, nodding in Chernow's direction. There were some chuckles from the gallery and some smiles from the jury, but the Judge didn't notice Chernow sitting there looking as if he was busting his bladder.

"I say we press on, Your Honor," Chernow insisted.

"Just didn't want anyone getting green, Your Honor."

Several members of the jury laughed. They had noticed. The judge looked at the wall clock.

"Indeed it is time for the break," said the Judge. "Court will be in recess for fifteen minutes."

Normally Brent would not want to give the opposition any extra time to work on their cross, but, in this case, he didn't care because he knew that there was nothing that Brad could throw at

Nancy that she could not handle, and he wanted the testimony she had just given to ferment.

* * *

Nancy sat back in the witness box, all lonely and afraid. She remembered what Brent had told her. Just tell the truth and everything will work out. But she just couldn't wait to get off that stand and out of that courtroom.

"Mrs. Haskins," asked Chernow, "Isn't it true that you didn't like Ms. Densmore?"

"Yes, I already said that."

"You hated her, didn't you, Mrs. Haskins?"

"No, I didn't hate her. She just wasn't one of my favorite people. Whenever I had contact with her it was never pleasant."

"Move to strike after "No I didn't hate her" Your Honor."

"Denied. Please continue."

"In fact, you blamed Ms. Densmore for the foreclosure on your house, didn't you?"

"No, as I said before, I knew I was behind on my assessments. It was nobody's fault but mine.

I just think she should have tried to work it out with me."

"Move to strike as non-responsive, Your Honor."

"Granted. Answer the question please, Mrs. Haskins."

"Can you repeat the question, please?"

"Yes, you blamed Ms. Densmore for the foreclosure on your home, didn't you?"

"No, I did not. I didn't like her intolerance and lack of compassion."

"Move to strike after "No I did not," Your Honor."

"Denied."

"You knew it was Ms. Densmore's birthday, didn't you?"

"No, how would I know that?" Nancy looked genuinely surprised at that question.

"And on that day, you had a bouquet of flowers delivered to Ms. Densmore, isn't that correct?"

"No, it is not. Absolutely not."

Chernow knew that Nancy would deny it, of course. He was just trying to crack her credibility in front of the jury. Brent hoped that he didn't crack her completely.

"And you rigged the flower food package to explode with deadly ricin, isn't that correct?"

"No, I did no such thing. Before this court case, I didn't even know what ricin was." Nancy looked at the jury as if she was pleading for help.

"You never watched *Breaking Bad*?" asked Chenow.

"What's that?" Nancy asked, innocently. Two of the men in the jury chuckled and all of the women looked surprised. They had obviously never seen *Breaking Bad* either. Chernow continued, flustered.

"And then, after the ambulance left with Ms. Densmore in it, you broke into her house, and took away all evidence of the poisoning, isn't that true, Mrs. Haskins?"

"I did no such thing. God knows it, and I think in your heart of hearts, you know it too, Mr. Chernow." *Point for Nancy,* thought Brent.

"Your Honor! Move to strike as non-responsive."

"The answer will be stricken and the jury is to disregard everything after *I did no such thing.*"

"You cleaned up every trace of ricin at Ms. Densmore's house, didn't you, Mrs. Haskins?"

"I did *not*!"

"And you removed the cellophane and package that was contaminated with ricin and threw it away in your own garbage can, didn't you Mrs. Haskins?"

"No, I did not. I swear it!" Nancy was holding her own. The poor girl didn't crack.

Chernow wore Nancy down, varying his questions around the same deadly theme until he finally had shot his load and stopped.

"Redirect?" Brent had been saving the best for last.

"Thank you, Your Honor."

"Mrs. Haskins, how did you feel when you won the action to set aside the foreclosure?"

"Objection, irrelevant and outside the scope of cross examination." Chernow had given Brent a gift. He argued his objection in front of the jury.

"Your Honor, it is inside the scope and I am entitled to examine Mrs. Haskins state of mind. Her elation after the foreclosure was off eliminates any criminal intent."

"Your Honor!" Chernow protested.

"Overruled, you may answer."

"I felt relieved. It was like all was good in the world again. I was happy for the first time since Burt was alive. I was so... happy!" Nancy started to cry. The Judge whispered to the clerk, who gave her box of Kleenex to the Bailiff and he delivered it to Nancy.

"Thank you," she said, taking a Kleenex from the box and wiping her eyes. "I can't believe this is happening!" More tears. Every member of the jury looked like they wanted to hug Nancy.

"Your Honor, there is no question pending," said the heartless Chernow.

"Do you need a break, Mrs. Haskins?"

Say no! Say no! thought Brent.

"No, I'm alright."

"Mrs. Haskins, given the fact that you were so happy, what thoughts, if any, did you have for Ms. Densmore?"

"Only good thoughts for everyone. I was so relieved, there was nothing that anyone could do to get me down. I was finally back on a positive track, with a plan how to resolve all my financial worries. Then this." She clenched her wadded

Kleenex and looked up at the ceiling, as if to ask God why he slammed her with this after everything was going so well.

"No further questions, Your Honor. The defense rests."

"Thank you Gentlemen. You may step down Mrs. Haskins. Ladies and gentlemen of the jury, we are going to recess for the day so the lawyers and I can go over jury instructions.

"Let me give you ladies and gentlemen an idea of what will happen tomorrow. The People will give their closing argument, then the defense. Then the People will give their rebuttal to the defense argument. Then I will read all of the instructions regarding the law to apply to the evidence you have heard in this case. You don't have to worry about taking notes, because a copy of all the instructions will be made available to you in the jury room. Have a good afternoon and we will see you back here at 9:00 a.m. sharp tomorrow."

* * *

It was a quiet evening, quite a contrast to the hectic and strenuous day in court. Brent reviewed all the notes of the trial, while Angela took care of him and the cat. It was like they had been living together for years.

"You're going to do great tomorrow, honey, I know you are," said Angela, as they hit the pillows.

CHAPTER THIRTY-SEVEN

The jurors filed in and took their seats in the crowded courtroom. Today was the day of final argument, a lawyer's masterpiece theater. Today there would be no witnesses, no cross examinations, only raw combat between two legal gladiators. There would be no choice of weapons in this Coliseum. The weapons were words, which they would hurl at each other with precision, like smart bombs.

"Ladies and gentlemen, said the Judge. "You have heard the evidence and now you will hear the arguments of the attorneys. Please keep in mind what I told you at the beginning of this trail. Argument is not evidence and you must not consider it as such. Mr. Chernow, you may make your final argument," said the Judge.

"Thank you, Your Honor," Chernow said, as he approached the jury box confidently, like a boxer stepping into the ring. He put his notes on the podium that had been set in front of them.

"Ladies and gentlemen, you have patiently listened to all the evidence in this trial. First, I would like to say that it is understandable that you may have compassion for the defendant. You may think that she is otherwise a nice lady. But remember this – you have a very important responsibility here. You are making the decision in this case. Our society cannot peacefully exist if people are allowed to kill each other, and whether you think you like a person or not, if he or she has committed murder, you twelve people, sitting as a jury, cannot let your emotions get in the way of your duty.

"Remember what I told you in the opening statement, that a trial was like a puzzle? You now must consider all of the evidence you heard and saw, and put that puzzle together. Most of it was circumstantial evidence, but a case may be proven by circumstantial evidence. As the judge will instruct you, circumstantial evidence is evidence that does not directly prove a fact to be decided, but is evidence of another fact or group of facts from which you may logically and reasonably conclude the truth of the fact in question.

"The Judge will also instruct you on the elements of murder by poison. He will tell you that ricin is a poison. If you find that the defendant intended to kill Barbara Densmore and you find that she was killed with poison, you must return a verdict for first degree murder with special circumstances.

"Let's talk about the poison first. The People have shown beyond any reasonable doubt, that Barbara Densmore was killed by the administration of ricin from a package that contained flowers that were delivered on her birthday. How do we know this? We have expert testimony from Dr. Perez that ricin poisoning was the cause of death. The actual packaging which contained this lethal ricin bomb was found at the defendant's house inside the defendant's garage.

"Fingerprints of Barbara Densmore were all over the cellophane wrapping, so the only reasonable and logical conclusion you can draw from that is that this was the murder weapon, because even just a small amount of ricin can kill you. You have heard the testimony of our expert who stated that the package containing the ricin exploded like bomb when Ms. Densmore opened it. And the only reasonable and logical conclusion you can draw from the fact that the packaging was found in the defendant's home is that she put it there after she cleaned the crime scene. It was in her possession and control and there is no contradictory evidence to draw any other inference of how it got there."

Chernow continued, pausing to quench his drying mouth with water, and then pushed on, arguing every facet of his case. It was a thorough, but boring argument. Boring because he covered every single piece of evidence and testimony, as he felt he had to. Thorough, but too detailed and clinical. Nevertheless, the jury appeared to be following him. After all, nothing he was saying was anything they had not heard before.

Brent took notes during Chernow's argument to make sure that he would address everything that Chernow had said when it was his turn to argue. Chernow had two opportunities to address the jury, but Brent would have only one. He had anticipated everything he thought Chernow would say in making his outline, but he needed to be sure that every point that Chernow made was addressed and argued. He also paid attention to the jury as Chernow continued to argue.

"Now let's talk about intent to kill, the other element of the charge of murder by poison. Ricin is a deadly poison. The act of rigging the ricin to explode in Barbara Densmore's face was a willful act, not an accident. It was a conscious act, in disregard for human life, and calculated to deliver a lethal penalty. Before this deadly gift was delivered, Nancy Haskins had the opportunity to think about it and decide to back out of her murderous plan. She could have called the delivery off at any time. She could have run over to Barbara's house and taken the flowers away. But she didn't change her mind. This shows deliberation, ladies and gentlemen. She knew that ricin would most likely kill Barbara Densmore, or anyone who opened them. Her plan was to kill Ms. Densmore. Why else would she deliver flowers laced with one of the deadliest poisons known to man?

Chernow continued his argument all the way to the lunch hour, using all of his allotted time, so his words could percolate along with the juror's coffee and sit in their brains as they munched on their ham and cheese sandwiches. He stepped around and in front of the podium to cast his final spell.

"Ladies and gentlemen, the evidence leads to only one reasonable and logical conclusion. The People have proven beyond a reasonable doubt that the defendant…"

Chernow paused, turned to Nancy and pointed his finger at her, just in case the jury had forgotten who the accused actually was.

"...Nancy Haskins did willfully, deliberately, in conscious disregard of human life, and with premeditation, murder Barbara Densmore by poison. You have a sworn duty to find her guilty of murder in the first degree with the special circumstance of murder by poison. Thank you."

Chernow took one last, serious look at the jury and then confidently walked back to the counsel table and took his seat.

"The Court will be in recess. See you back here at 1:30. Ladies and gentlemen, I remind you again that you may not discuss the case with anyone else, or amongst yourselves."

CHAPTER THIRTY-EIGHT

Brent approached the lectern and set down his outline, which was all marked up from the notes he had taken during Chernow's final argument. He had to cover his original material, and all those notes, including everything he had anticipated that Chernow would say in his rebuttal, because this was the last chance Brent would have to make his plea to the jury.

"Ladies and gentlemen of the jury, good afternoon. You have heard and seen all of the evidence that the People have to present in this case. Lawyers are sometimes known as "mouthpieces."

Brent saw that most of the men on the jury were smiling at this comment. He was happy that he could hit an empathetic note with them. After all, they were the captive audience.

"And now is the time when we engage in the fantasy that anything we may have to say about this case may make a difference in how you make your decision. Since you've already heard all the evidence that the People have presented, there should be nothing more to say. This case is not a boxing match between myself and Mr. Chernow where you award the winner based on which jabs connected and which didn't. It's not a game show, and your verdict isn't a price that goes to the wittiest contestant."

Brent put up his finger, and wagged it at the jury as he continued.

"No, no. The stakes here are far graver than that. Your decision determines the fate of this kind old lady who is a stranger to all of you. You will probably never see her after today, never touch each other's lives again in any way, but the decision that you make today will impact her for the rest of her life.

"You will be instructed by the Judge that, in order to find Nancy Haskins guilty of murder in the first degree, you must find, beyond a reasonable doubt that the evidence shows she intended to kill Barbara Densmore. You must also find, without a reasonable doubt, that she did in fact kill Ms. Densmore, and, in order to find the special circumstances that Nancy Haskins committed murder by poison, you must find, beyond a reasonable doubt, that she used poison to kill Barbara Densmore. In this case, ladies and gentlemen, it is impossible for you to come to those conclusions."

Brent left the podium, stood in front of the jury box, and continued.

"In order for you to examine each piece of evidence through this looking glass of reasonable doubt, you have to know what it means first. What does it mean when the Judge tells you that reasonable doubt doesn't require that every doubt has to be erased from your mind? To make a finding beyond a reasonable doubt means that you have to be convinced in *your own mind* that the fact is true to an abiding conviction. That is what the law says, but does anyone know what that means? I know that a lot of kids believe in Santa Claus to an abiding conviction…"

There were some smiles and chuckles from the jury box. Brent took a sip of water from the cup on the podium and continued.

"I know that many people believe in God to an abiding conviction, and that some people don't. This is a very difficult task, you see.

"The Judge will tell you that reasonable doubt is not imaginary, it's not what you think may be possible, but a fair doubt in your mind, that leaves you, after careful examination of all the evidence, in a state where you cannot say with an abiding conviction to a moral certainty that the particular element or charge against the defendant has been proven. But there's no mystery about your role here. You have to question every piece of evidence, with your minds and with your hearts, to decide whether you have that abiding conviction or not. There is no other way to do it.

"Think of this trial like an airplane. Most of you have probably been on an airplane and you know that you are entrusting your lives to the pilot every time you fly. The pilot is given a route to follow, and the computer of the plane can probably do most of the work for him, but the pilot is the one who looks out the window and constantly checks all the instruments to make sure that he or she sees just where the plane is going and that everything is in proper working order."

"I think most of us who have flown have had to sit on the tarmac or even get off the plane because the pilot found that an instrument is not working correctly, or an indicator light is out of order. After all, he or she is responsible for the lives of the passengers, just as you ladies and gentlemen are responsible for this important decision.

The pilot has to decide whether or not it is safe to take off. If he or she decides that visibility is too poor, or that the aircraft is not sound enough to take off, that plane is not going anywhere."

Brent crossed his arms at the wrists in front of himself, bringing them apart, like an umpire giving the "safe" signal at second base.

"It is only when the pilot decides, *to an abiding conviction*, that all systems are go, that the plane will take off. Otherwise, it stays on the ground, and everyone gets off. If the pilot has a reasonable doubt as to the safety of the plane, it will stay on the tarmac until that doubt has been resolved or a substitute plane is brought in. You, ladies and gentlemen, are the pilots in this case. If you have a reasonable doubt, as to an abiding conviction, about any element of the prosecution's case, it is your duty to acquit Nancy Haskins. She comes into this Court, presumed as an innocent woman, and this case stands or falls entirely on what the People have presented.

"Let's talk about Mr. Chernow's puzzle analogy. Each piece of evidence that he presented is a piece of that puzzle. If you find that any one element of the People's case – any one piece of the puzzle – has not been proven beyond a reasonable doubt, you must find Nancy Haskins not guilty, *even if you think that she might be guilty*. Your decision is not whether *you* think she is guilty or not. What you *feel* about her innocence or guilt does not come into the equation. It is whether you think that the prosecution has proven every element it must prove beyond a reasonable doubt that you must decide. I am going to point out to you what pieces are missing in the puzzle and why the prosecution has not met its burden of proof.

"If the elements of this case are pieces in the puzzle, then you must examine each one to ascertain if it has been proven beyond a reasonable doubt. The first piece of the puzzle is the cause of death. Mr. Chernow says it was caused by poisoning. You may think that this is an easy part, but it's not. The only way to clinically prove that it was ricin that killed Barbara Densmore is a urine test on a sample that was sent to CDC and thereafter sent out to their Laboratory Network. Neither this sample, nor any test confirming any ricin in the sample is in evidence, so we must assume that no positive results exist.

"Dr. Perez says that there is another way to confirm ricin poisoning, and that is to look for ricin in the environment or vicinity of where the death occurred. You've heard testimony that the death occurred at Barbara Densmore's home, which is three blocks away from Nancy Haskins' home. You've heard testimony that *no ricin was found* on Barbara Densmore's clothes; nor was any ricin found in her house – *none*! You've heard testimony from Dr. Orozco, who is also a medical examiner, that Ms. Densmore's symptoms are the same symptoms one would expect from a patient with tracheal or lung cancer, or influenza, one of the most common causes of death in the United States."

Brent moved to the white board, and drew a "1" and a "2."

"The Judge will instruct you that, if there are two reasonable inferences you can draw from the evidence, one of which leads to the conclusion that Mrs. Haskins is guilty, and one of which leads to the conclusion that she is *not* guilty, that you must select the inference that leads to the conclusion that she is not guilty. One inference is death by poison," said Brent, as he wrote death by poison next to the number 1. "The other inference is either cancer or influenza," which Brent wrote next to number 2, and turned back to face the jury.

"Both of these inferences are supported by the evidence in the autopsy and toxicology reports. You must pick number 2 – cancer or influenza – because that is the inference that leads to the conclusion that Nancy Haskins is not guilty. Therefore, this element, death by poison, has not been proven beyond a reasonable doubt.

"Let's look at the cellophane wrapping and flower food package. The evidence shows that these items were contaminated with ricin. No doubt about that. It also shows that Barbara Densmore's fingerprints were on the wrapping. No doubt about that. What it doesn't show is when the ricin got into the packaging. Was it before or after Barbara Densmore handled it?

"What the evidence also doesn't show is who put the packaging in Nancy Haskins' trash can. Mr. Chernow's going to tell you that this is the smoking gun. This is his entire case! Ladies and gentlemen, if you decide this is the gun, there is a huge problem, and that problem is that there are *no fingerprints* of the perpetrator on the gun.

"There's an even bigger problem than that. The wrapping was found in an unsecured garage that was open to anyone who opened the unlocked side door. If someone was intending to frame Mrs. Haskins, this is the perfect way to do it. It doesn't make sense that Mrs. Haskins would thoroughly clean the crime scene of every trace of ricin, dispose of the flowers that were never found, and then dispose of the last piece of incriminating evidence in her own trash can.

"Finally, Dr. Medina seems to think that any high school science student can make ricin, but, Ladies and gentlemen, Nancy Haskins is a 73 year old lady. Whipping up a batch of ricin poison from instructions on the Internet is not like following a recipe for chocolate chip cookies. There was no evidence of an oil press, protective clothing or anything found in her home. Only the cellophane wrapping and flower food package that had to have been planted by someone else.

Brent took to the white board again and drew another "1" and "2." "Mr. Chernow wants you to draw an inference from the evidence that Nancy Haskins put the packaging in her own trash can, in an open garage, with gloves on so she would not leave fingerprints," Brent said, as he wrote next to number 1, then looked in the direction of Chernow, who was taking copious notes. The jurors looked at Chernow too. Brent had their attention.

"Then you have to ask yourself *where are the flowers?* And *why would Nancy put the wrapping in her own trash can if she was careful enough to not leave any fingerprints?* It would seem to me that someone who is calculating enough to whip up a batch of ricin, and rig it so that it would blow up in Ms. Densmore's face would be too sophisticated to dump the flowers in one place that the police would never find, and throw the wrapping in her own trash can. The other reasonable inference you can draw from this evidence is that *someone else went into the open garage and put the cellophane wrap there*," argued Brent, as he wrote next to number 2 on the board. "Therefore, this element has not been proven beyond a reasonable doubt."

Brent could see the older women in the jury almost nodding in agreement to his argument. He poured himself another cup of water and continued.

"And what about Nancy's testimony? Remember, she doesn't have to prove anything, and she especially doesn't have to prove that she *didn't* do anything. But she did testify, under oath, and her testimony is evidence that you must consider, that she did *not* kill Barbara Densmore and she did *not* handle the contaminated wrapping.

"Remember the airplane analogy? There are too many pieces of the puzzle that are covered in reasonable doubt. So covered in it, it's impossible to see the entire picture. Ladies and gentlemen, I ask you, if your pilot could see this out of the windshield of the cockpit, would you want to get on that plane?" Brent took a piece of paper out of his pocket, unfolded it and held it up between himself and the jury like a mask. The piece of paper had holes torn in it, and through the holes, the jurors could hardly see Brent's face. He panned the paper in front of the jury box.

"I don't think so. What about Felipe Corral and Gary Goldstein, who refused to testify on the grounds it may *incriminate* them? We know that Mr. Goldstein has an anger problem, and has had arguments with Ms. Densmore. We know that Corral is suspected of smuggling drugs, that he has assaulted my investigator, Jack Ruder, and that Ms. Densmore was always snooping around his house, looking for violations.

"As I told you before, ladies and gentlemen, this is not a game – it is not a puzzle. And you know in your minds and your hearts that the prosecution has not proven its case beyond a reasonable doubt. You have only one choice, and that is to find Nancy Haskins *not guilty* of murder in the first degree, *not guilty* of the lesser included charge of second degree murder, and that the special circumstance of murder by poison has *not* been proven beyond a reasonable doubt. Thank you."

There was muffled applause coming from the gallery. Brent went to gather his notes, and realized that, out of the 30 pages of notes he had taken, he never got past page 5. He took his seat at counsel table with Nancy.

"That was a great argument, Brent," she said, with tears glistening in her eyes.

"Mr. Chernow?"

Bradley Chernow took the podium, set down his notes and began his rebuttal.

"Ladies and gentlemen, Mr. Marks is a very, very clever lawyer. After all, this is a very serious matter. Serious to his case, to be sure, but also serious to the People of the State of California. This isn't a jungle we live in. And the reason it's not a jungle is because we live by laws here. In our society of laws, there must be punishment to prohibit the act of murder. If there is not, then there would be no safety on our streets. The Judge will tell you that reasonable doubt does not mean the erasure of all doubts in your mind. *You may have doubts!* But, looking at all the evidence as a whole, you should have no reasonable doubt – you should have an abiding conviction that the defendant is guilty.

"Look at the inference Mr. Marks wants you to draw about the cellophane wrapping. The evidence shows that the wrapping was found in the garbage can inside of Nancy Haskins' garage, not anyone else's garage, and not on the street. *Her* garage in *her* home," he declared as he pointed his finger at Nancy.

"As I told you before, there is hardly ever direct evidence of a crime. As Dr. Medina testified, finding out how to make ricin is as easy as looking up *ricin* on the Internet. And anyone can buy castor beans to make the ricin. If Nancy Haskins had enough malice and forethought to kill Barbara Densmore, which she did, a few details such as protective clothing and an oil press were not going to stop her.

"There is no evidence at all that has been presented that anyone else put the plastic wrap in the garbage from which you may draw that inference number two. Inference number two doesn't exist. The only evidence of inference number two is the defendant saying, *I didn't do it!* Ladies and gentlemen, the prisons are filled with defendants who said they didn't do it. That is not evidence from which you can draw an inference that someone else put it there. There is absolutely *no* evidence that anyone other than the defendant may have put it there."

Brent was truly worried now. Not only was Chernow's argument coherent and on point, it actually made sense. In all of his preparation, Brent had tried to realize all the weaknesses in his case. Perhaps he was too zealous in his representation to realize them. He knew that Nancy was innocent, he felt it in his heart, but maybe she would have been better off with a lawyer who wasn't convinced of her innocence. Maybe the truth really wouldn't set her free.

Brent had always told his clients that *you can be convicted of anything.* Maybe it was true. The prosecution's job was to seek convictions. The District Attorney was an elected position and more convictions meant more votes. The prosecution didn't care what the truth really was – it cared what *its truth was.* The police and the D.A. worked so closely together as "law enforcement" that there was almost an unwritten code to mislead. Brent had often caught cops on the witness stand "filling in the blanks." That's why lawyers always advised clients to never talk to the police. When they say whatever you say may be used against you, they mean it! Once they have decided who to go after, they do it like an assassin's assignment. Brent held on Chernow's argument attentively.

"If the defendant threw the wrapping in the trash, and there was ricin on it, and Barbara Densmore's fingerprints were on it, the only inference you can draw from this evidence is that this was the package which contained the deadly poison that killed her and that the defendant put it there. The fact that it had the victim's fingerprints on it is enough to confirm Dr. Perez' diagnosis of ricin poisoning *no matter where it was found.*

"Ladies and gentlemen, don't be fooled by the trickery of the defense and Mr. Marks' props. The People have proven beyond a reasonable doubt that Nancy Haskins," he said, pointing at her again, "murdered Barbara Densmore with poison, and you must return a verdict of murder in the first degree with special circumstances."

The hush in the courtroom turned into a collective sigh, then the murmur of whispered conversation took over.

"Order, order," said the Judge.

"Quiet in the courtroom please," said the Bailiff.

CHAPTER THIRTY-NINE

Judge Curtis proceeded to read the instructions to the jury, verbatim, which dragged on for an hour. The audience in the gallery was fairly disappointed and bored, and most of them cleared out, except, of course, for Frances Templeton.

The Judge carefully read and explained the definition of murder, the difference between first and second degree murder, the presumption of innocence, and the principle of reasonable doubt.

The jurors tried to follow the instructions, but began nodding off after the first half hour. When the Judge had finished reading the instructions, he excused the alternate jurors and sent the jury to the jury room to deliberate.

"Mr. Brandon and Mrs. Heath, you are both excused as alternate jurors. If for some reason, one of the jurors is not able to serve, we will recall you. I would like to thank you for your time and your service."

Suddenly, a feeling of exhaustion overwhelmed Brent, so much so that he felt like crawling under the counsel table and taking a nap.

Nancy hugged Brent as he was packing up. "I don't know how to thank you," she said, with tears streaking down her cheeks. "What happens next?"

"We wait for the verdict," said Brent.

Bradley Chernow paused between the counsel tables and shook Brent's hand.

"Good job, counselor," Brent said.

"Thank you," Chernow replied, and left. Perhaps it was the fatigue of the battle, or maybe he finally realized that this was not a personal contest, and that Brent was not a grandstander, just a lawyer like he was.

After Brent briefed the reporters for about half an hour, and they cleared out, he said good bye to Nancy and Jillian and trudged out of the Courthouse.

As Brent ambled down the corridor, with vision of a nice warm bed dancing in his head, that little gnat Frances Templeton came up to him and touched him on the sleeve.

"Can I talk to you?"

"Frances, I don't think we have anything to say to each other."

"I just want to ask you a question."

Brent stopped dead in his tracks, and put down his briefcase next to his rolling case of trial notebooks.

"What?" he asked, with impatience.

"It's a legal question."

Great, thought Brent. He was always the most sought after person at the party, because everyone wanted to ask a free legal question. It was usually my brother or sister, this and that, and always a waste of Brent's time.

"What's the question?" he asked, against his better judgment.

"It's completely confidential."

"Yeah, yeah." Brent was too tired to argue, and all he wanted to do was escape.

"If I killed somebody, and then framed the murder on someone else, could I be tried for both crimes, and what kinds of defenses should I use?"

Brent instantly felt a pain in his gut, like someone had kicked him in the stomach with their boots on. He just stared at Frances, open mouthed and in shock.

"And if you represented the person I framed, would it be a conflict of interest?" she added, innocently, batting her eyelashes.

"You bitch!"

"Come now Brent, is that all the brilliant white hot lawyer Brent Marks can say? You bitch?"

Suddenly Brent realized. "You cooked the books, didn't you? You were skimming money from the Association and you cooked the books! No wonder they were so perfect! They're all fake! You had to kill Barbara because she knew!"

"It's over Brent, win or lose. They're sure that Nancy did it. If they fry her, the case is closed. If they acquit her, the case is closed."

"What makes you think that?"

"Your buddy Chernow told me."

Frances thought she had it all figured out, and she probably did.

"Just remember Brent, whatever I tell you is attorney client privileged. I checked. It'll always be our little secret."

With that, Frances blew Brent a kiss, turned around and left.

Brent felt doubled over, as if he were wounded. This despicable practice of criminal law. No wonder he didn't want to do it anymore. He remembered the classes he had taken on legal ethics. Those "legal questions" at parties were enough to make you the lawyer of the drunken fool who had asked the question, and real liability always attached to that. By the same token, once the veil of confidence was invoked, the attorney client privilege attached.

Brent was trapped, pushed against the corner by a murderess and imprisoned there by the attorney client privilege, something he had taken an oath to preserve and a mantra that he had lived by for over 20 years. He now questioned the very existence of his profession, and his choice of it as his own. If Nancy should be condemned and he held the key to her prison cell, would he ever be able to live with himself?

CHAPTER FORTY

Brent went back to the office. There was nothing more to do except wait for the jury. The court would call, and then he and Nancy would get down to the courthouse for the final chapter in the case of People v. Haskins. He thought about going into the office later, but it had been neglected for so long, he headed straight there.

An enormous pile of mail was stacked on his desk, opened and with sticky notes that Melinda had placed on some of the more important ones. That stack competed with one smaller in volume, but equal in number of phone messages, also with sticky notes. As Brent went through the messages, he had a wrestling match in his mind over the attorney-client privilege. The attorney-client privilege covered any communication between an attorney and his client. It didn't matter that Frances had not paid him, because she had asked for legal advice, and that made him her lawyer in the eyes of the law. It was the trap that every ethics course always teaches a lawyer to watch out for. They always say, *don't talk to people at parties – you'll end up in a malpractice suit someday* – and Brent had fallen right into it. But the privilege only prohibited Brent from revealing communications. He was prohibited from ever revealing what Frances had told him outside the courtroom.

Finally, when Brent realized that neither his brain nor his body could stand to be in the office one minute longer, he went home. When he arrived, he was happy to see Angela's car parked out front. Whether it was good news or bad news, she was the one he always wanted to tell first. Brent crossed the portal to his beloved home a weary soldier, coming home from the war.

"You look like you could use a drink," was the first thing Angela said. Brent merely nodded. Once he had shelved his battle gear, he sunk into the couch and made his confession.

"I'm really stuck now, Angie."

"Because of the case?" she asked, handing him a glass of Bailey's on the rocks.

"No, because of attorney-client privilege. I can't even tell you about it."

"Is there someone you can talk to?"

"No," he said, swishing the coffee color liquid over the ice cubes. "This is something I have to figure out by myself. In the old days, I could talk to Charles about it, because he was my associate, but now it's just me."

Angela looked at Brent with compassionate eyes. "I know you'll do the right thing."

"That's just it, Angie. I have to do the right thing, but do it without doing the wrong thing."

"Sounds like a bar exam question."

"It is," Brent said, realizing how well she comprehended without knowing all the detail. She always did. In all the relationships Brent had had before, nobody had the understood him as well as Angela did.

While Angela was busy preparing dinner, Brent sat on the balcony, looked out over the ocean from the harbor to the horizon. *What would you do, Charles?* He thought. Then, after a while, the answer came to him. Just like that.

CHAPTER FORTY-ONE

When psychiatrists talk about stress, they really have no idea what they are talking about unless they have been through the ordeal of a trial. Waiting for a jury to render a verdict is the epitome of stress. On the instructions of Brent, Nancy stayed home and waited for his call, but Brent visited the courtroom every day and stayed there as long as possible. It was like watching the proverbial pot and waiting for it to boil.

The jury room had a buzzer that they could ring if they had a question, or if they had finally come to a verdict. Every time that buzzer rang in the courtroom Brent literally jumped out of his skin, and it would inevitably be that someone had to go to the bathroom or they wanted an early lunch break. A couple of times, they asked questions, and both lawyers were called in to discuss the question with the Judge and provide an answer, if possible, to pass on to the jury.

But one day, Melinda called Brent on his cell phone and told him he was needed in court right away, and that Nancy's presence was required as well. When Brent, Nancy and Jillian arrived almost simultaneously, the Bailiff brought the jurors in, and they filed into their seats. Brent examined their faces. They were a mixture of exhaustion and what also looked like disappointment.

Judge Curtis declared, "Ladies and gentlemen, your foreman tells me you are hopelessly deadlocked, is that correct?"

"Yes, Your Honor, said the Foreman, a Chief Accountant for a large accounting firm.

"And do you think that more time would help you reach a unanimous verdict?"

"No, Your Honor," said the Foreman. "We are at an impasse. I'm afraid it's impossible."

"Then I would like to thank you on behalf of the State of California and the County of Santa Barbara for your service. Jury service is imperative to the functioning of a democracy, and we are in your debt. You all are discharged. You may stay, if you wish, and speak to the lawyers. The admonishment against speaking to them is now lifted. I caution you, however, against speaking about this case with anyone else, because the People may decide to refile."

"What does it mean?" asked Nancy.

"It's a hung jury. They can't decide," answered Brent.

"The defendant is released and discharged and her bail is exonerated," said the Judge.

Jillian cried, and hugged Nancy with relief. Brent explained to Nancy that the D.A. would now have to decide whether to file again or not. If they did, there would be another trial. If they didn't, the nightmare would be over. Nancy was disappointed, surprised, and upset, but she realized the job Brent had done and thanked him. She was free. *Frances didn't anticipate a hung jury,* thought Brent. This may open the investigation up again, to try to plug the holes in the prosecution's case.

Brent stayed behind to speak to the jury. He usually hated that part, but, in the event he had to try the case again, he thought he could benefit from their thinking process. Only a few jurors stayed to discuss the case, and there were no great revelations.

After speaking to the jury, Brent and Chernow stayed on to discuss the case with the reporters. When the crowd had dissipated, only Brent and Chernow were left standing.

"Want to go for a beer?" asked Brent.

Chernow hesitated, then said, "Why not?"

The Pressroom was an authentic English pub, with wood paneling soaked with the smell of beer and decorated with British flags, barrels and old framed pictures. That suited Chernow just fine, because it was just the place to order his favorite Guinness on tap. Brent toasted his mug with his usual Corona.

"Brad, if you're thinking about refiling this case…"

"Whoa, is that why you asked me for a beer? To talk me out of refiling?"

"Calm down, Brad. That's not why. What you decide to do is up to you and the D.A.'s office. I just wanted to suggest something."

"What do you know?"

The comment was as if Chernow had a feeling that there was something missing all along. Something that Brent knew and he didn't.

"Actually Brad, I can't tell you what I know. But I am an officer of the court and, as such, I took an oath to this system and I want to see that justice is done."

"Go ahead."

"When you do your post-mortem of this case, go over the books and records of the Orange Grove Homeowner's Association and compare them with the banking records. I think you'll figure out your next step from there."

EPILOGUE

Brent sat in the last row of Frances Templeton's trial every day, just as she had sat in on Nancy's. When the jury returned a verdict of "guilty," he silently smiled to himself. And, when the Bailiff took Frances by the arm into custody, she turned her head and shouted out, "I know it was you, Marks! I'll have you disbarred!"

Brent said nothing in return. He just sat and watched as the Bailiff slapped the handcuffs on Frances and dragged her away. Justice had finally been done.

AFTERWORD

Of course, most people don't murder the heads of their homeowner's association. But covenants and restrictions have turned many formerly pesky neighbors into mini despots. If you care to read on, I have summarized some of the research I have done for this novel. If not, I would like to ask you now to please leave a review. Finally, I love to get email from my readers. Please feel free to send me one at info@kennetheade.com. I would also like you to join my mailing list, for advance notice of new books, free excerpts, free books and updates. I will never spam you. Please subscribe here: http://bit.do/mailing-list.

This story is fiction, but two cases of HOA hell gave it inspiration. The first was Sammi Goldstein. Sammi had gone through more trials in life than most of her neighbors in the quiet bedroom community of Stevenson Ranch, north of Los Angeles, California. Her daughter Stephanie suffered for years from IBD. Sammi fought for her daughter's life through 16 agonizing surgeries at the best hospitals in the country. But the trial that really broke her down was the one she was never allowed to attend until she had to defend herself from a contempt of court charge. You could say it was a case of color. When her homeowner's association, Southern Oaks Society, asked Sammi to paint her house, she complied by painting it almost the exact same color as a neighbor with the same tract model, with the exception of a blue door and shutters. But, according to Southern Oaks, the color was all wrong. So wrong, that they sued Sammi for it, and got a judgment against her without her even knowing about it.

While Sammi was in Minnesota at the Mayo Clinic during several of her daughter's surgeries, the HOA served her husband, with whom she was separated at the time, with the summons and complaint, took Sammi's default and she didn't find out about it until the HOA wiped her children's savings accounts out to the tune of $5,000, on an assessment and attorney's fee bill of over $50,000. The HOA finally did succeed in personally serving Sammi, but it was with a contempt of court citation, threatening her with imprisonment if she didn't repaint her house. I succeeded in getting the default judgment set aside, and the case eventually settled.

Homeowner's Associations in California continue to badger homeowners with infractions of rules and regulations under the authority of Civil Code section 1354, which entitles them to enforce deed restrictions as equitable servitudes.

HOA's should be mindful of the principle that "one who seeks equity must do equity" and the equitable relief must be fashioned with the equitable rights of the defendant in mind. *Dickson, Carlson and Capillo v. Pole* (2000) 83 Cal. App. 4th 436 at 445-446. This principle makes a perfect shield against outrageous fines and fees. Homeowners facing adverse action from their HOA's should suggest reasonable equitable remedies to the Court that solve the problem without being punitive in nature.

Homeowner's Associations, created by deed provisions to serve homeowners in condominium developments, are often at odds with individual owners of units. Sometimes these conflicts escalate to the point where the HOA actually forecloses on a homeowner's interest in the unit, resulting in a total loss to the homeowner. In

California, the Davis-Stirling Common Interest Development Act, codified in Civil Code Sections 1350-1376, gives an HOA the authority to levy assessments, which become an involuntary lien against the homeowner's interest when the HOA records a "Notice of Delinquent Assessment" (Civil Code 1367). Section 1367(e) gives the HOA the right to enforce that lien in any manner permitted by law, including foreclosure. Thus, if the homeowner does not pay a delinquent assessment, his or her interest may be sold at either a judicial or non-judicial foreclosure sale, resulting in the possibility of the HOA becoming the owner of the unit and evicting the homeowner from their own home.

I recently came in to represent an elderly couple in Marina del Rey in such a case after a default judgment for judicial foreclosure. Thankfully, the legislature inserted stringent notice provisions in Civil Code 1367.1 by amendment in 2002 and 1367.4 by amendment in 2005, so I looked to them to ascertain whether there was compliance. The provisions require that, thirty days prior to recording a lien on the separate interest of any owner, the HOA must give notice by certified mail of its lien collection procedures, the method and calculation of the assessment amount, a statement that the owner has the right to inspect the HOA's records, and a specific warning that their interest may be sold without court action if the lien is placed in foreclosure (1367.1(a)(1). They also require an itemized statement of the assessments, late charges, collection and attorney's fees, a statement that the owner shall not be liable to pay the interest, charges, and costs of collection if it is determined that the assessment was paid on time, the right to request a meeting with the HOA board, the right to dispute the assessment by submitting a written request to the HOA for dispute resolution pursuant to its required "meet and confer" program, and the right to request alternative dispute resolution with a neutral third party (1367.1(a)(2-6). The decision to record the lien must be made by the HOA board by a majority vote (1367.1(c)(1)(B), and the notice of delinquent assessment must be recorded and a copy of the recorded notice served on the homeowner by certified mail. Section 1367.4 requires the HOA, prior to the use of foreclosure, to collect an assessment over $1800, to offer the "meet and confer," to make the decision to foreclose by a majority vote of the full HOA board, to provide notice of that decision to the owner by personal service, "in accordance with the manner of service of a summons (CCP sections 415.10, et. seq.), and to allow the homeowner a redemption period in cases of non-judicial foreclosure (Civil Code section 1367.4).

Prior to the case of *Diamond v. Superior Court,* 217 Cal. App. 4th 1172 (2013), decided by the Sixth District Court of Appeal on June 18, 2013, courts were refusing to overturn foreclosures if the HOA could demonstrate "substantial compliance" with the statute. The *Diamond* case held that the notice requirements of sections 1367.1 and 1367.4 must be strictly construed, "pursuant to the plain language of the statutes and their legislative history" and set aside the foreclosure sale in that case for the HOA's failure to send the homeowner a copy of the recorded notice of delinquent assessment and failing to give the required pre-lien notice of a right to demand alternative dispute resolution.

In my case, the homeowners came to me after a judicial foreclosure, on the verge of losing their home, in an attempt to stop the sale and force the HOA back to the bargaining table. The HOA in that case had not yet personally served the homeowner with a copy of the board's decision to foreclose on their home, and claimed that the statute did not specify when it should be served. Presumably, they could serve it any time before the foreclosure sale. However, the reason for personal service in accordance with CCP section 415.10 is to give notice of a legal process in order to comply with the principles of due process.

The fourteenth amendment to the United States Constitution provides that "no state shall deprive any person of life, liberty or property without due process of law." The legislative history of the amendment creating section 1367.4, plainly requires the HOA board to provide notice of its decision to foreclose as a condition of foreclosure, which is a taking of property authorized by the state. Notice is a concept of due process, and to require that notice to be given by personal service, as opposed to the other methods of service specified in the Code of Civil Procedure, the legislature plainly prescribed the highest form of notice. The purpose of such service statutes is to assure that due process is satisfied. See *American Express Centurion Bank v. Zara,* 199 Cal. App 4th 383 (2011). Clearly, since the statute specifies personal service of the board's decision as a precondition of foreclosure, that service must occur before the commencement of foreclosure proceedings, to allow the homeowner notice and the opportunity to defend against them. The case is still pending.

One more thing…

I hope you have enjoyed this book and I am thankful that you have spent the time to get to this point, which means that you must have received something from reading it. If you turn to the last page, Kindle will give you the opportunity to rate the book and share your thoughts through an automatic feed to your Facebook and Twitter accounts. If you believe your friends would enjoy this book, I would be honored if you would post your thoughts, and also leave a review on Amazon. [Click here](#) for the book link for your review.

Best regards,

Kenneth Eade

info@kennetheade.com

BONUS OFFER

Sign up for paperback discounts, advance sale notifications of this and other books and free stuff by clicking here: http://bit.do/mailing-list. I will never spam you.

ABOUT THE AUTHOR

Author Kenneth Eade, best known for his legal and political thrillers, practiced law for 30 years before publishing his first novel, "An Involuntary Spy." Eade, an up-and-coming author in the legal thriller and courtroom drama genre, has been described by critics as "one of our strongest thriller writers on the scene, and the fact that he draws his stories from the contemporary philosophical landscape is very much to his credit." Critics have also said that "his novels will remind readers of John Grisham, proving that Kenneth Eade deserves to be on the same lists with the world's greatest thriller authors."

Says Eade of the comparisons: "John Grisham is famous for saying that sometimes he likes to wrap a good story around an important issue. In all of my novels, the story and the important issues are always present."

Eade is known to keep in touch with his readers, offering free gifts and discounts to all those who sign up at his web site, www.kennetheade.com.

Made in the USA
Middletown, DE
14 July 2016